CRAZY HORSE

Illustrated by Meryl Henderson

CRAZY HORSE
Young War Chief

by George E. Stanley

ALADDIN PAPERBACKS

New York   London   Toronto   Sydney

To Gwen, Charles, James, and Andrea—my anchors—with love, George and Dad

ALADDIN PAPERBACKS
An imprint of Simon & Schuster Children's Publishing Division
1230 Avenue of the Americas, New York, NY 10020
Text copyright © 2005 by George E. Stanley
Illustrations copyright © 2005 by Meryl Henderson
All rights reserved, including the right of
reproduction in whole or in part in any form.
ALADDIN PAPERBACKS, CHILDHOOD OF FAMOUS AMERICANS,
and colophon are trademarks of Simon & Schuster, Inc.
Designed by Lisa Vega
The text of this book was set in New Caledonia.
Manufactured in the United States of America
First Aladdin Paperbacks edition October 2005
2 4 6 8 10 9 7 5 3 1
Library of Congress Control Number 2002107418
ISBN-13: 978-0-689-85746-1
ISBN-10: 0-689-85746-2

ILLUSTRATIONS

CONTENTS

The Great Sioux Nation

It was late September 1841. The tribes of the Great Sioux Nation had gathered at Bear Butte in the shadow of the Black Hills, in what is today the state of South Dakota. They came every autumn like this to see other family members, to renew friendships, and to share the news of what had happened to them in the preceding year.

Once the Sioux had been a woodland people. They made their home in the forests to the east, but when their enemies, the Ojibwas, got guns from the white men, the Sioux were forced to move west. Now the Great Plains were home to them. There was hardly a Sioux living who remembered the time before they had horses and followed the buffalo from early spring until the snows forced them into a permanent winter camp.

Now the worst of the summer heat had passed, and the pleasant breezes from the northwest had swept away all the thick dust that had been stirred up by the arrival of the tribes. But some of the men were worried that there might not be enough dried buffalo to feed all their people through the winter. They talked about going on more buffalo hunts. Most of the young people in the camp weren't thinking about that, though. They were too busy having fun.

At the southern edge of the encampment, ten-year-old Crooked Nose was having a footrace with some of his cousins. He was the first runner to reach the goal—Short Bull's tipi. Crooked Nose circled the tipi twice, then stopped in front of the opening flap. He watched his smaller cousins as they wove their way through the other tipis, hoping at least to win second place. Crooked Nose remembered when coming in second had been his goal too. Now he thought only about winning.

Crooked Nose's tribe was the Oglalas. The other tribes were the Two Kettles, the Brulés, the Hunkpapas, the Miniconjous, the Sans Arcs, and the Blackfeet. All of these tribes were made up of smaller hunting bands that lived apart from one another. Crooked Nose knew that not all the other Oglala bands were at the encampment yet.

Finally two of Crooked Nose's favorite cousins, Half Moon and One Moon, reached him, and fell at his feet laughing. "That was fun!" they kept saying over and over.

Instead of laughing with them, though, Crooked Nose thought about scolding them and telling them that they needed to be more serious about the race.

But the Sioux never did this to their children, Crooked Nose knew. The children were petted and fussed over by all their relatives. No adult ever punished them. The Sioux did not believe in spanking or whipping their children. If they did something wrong, the adults talked to them gently, never harshly, and asked them to stop.

"It was fun, but it is also one of the things that Sioux boys should do to test their strength, their endurance, and their willingness to suffer pain without complaining," Crooked Nose said, repeating what he had heard his father say many times. "You must never forget that, Cousins. You are also learning how to get food for the tribe by hunting the buffalo and how to protect the tribe from our enemies."

"The Crows and the Shoshones!" Half Moon and One Moon shouted.

Crooked Nose nodded. "And now the United States Army, which is slowly invading our hunting grounds," he added.

Half Moon and One Moon stopped laughing. Now they looked serious. Suddenly Crooked Nose felt proud that he made his cousins understand that they could have fun, yet at the same time do things that would help turn them into Sioux warriors.

Soon they would go on raids and come home with scalps of the enemies they killed and with the horses they had captured. With the other warriors, they would ride in a celebration circle around the village, telling about their victories and bragging about their own brave deeds. The women and the girls would shout their names proudly.

Crooked Nose was sure that his name would be shouted louder than the others. Little children, maybe even ones he had played with a few weeks before, would rush after him, begging him to play with them again. He would smile at them, but he would never again do as they asked, because he was now a proud Sioux warrior.

Finally the rest of Crooked Nose's cousins reached Short Bull's tipi. Almost immediately they started giggling and falling on the ground, but Half Moon and One Moon stopped them with the same talk that Crooked Nose had just given them. Crooked Nose smiled.

"Let's wrestle," One Moon said to the group. He turned to Crooked Nose. "Will you show us how?"

Crooked Nose had just opened his mouth to say that he would when he noticed his father, Two Bows, run out of their tipi and, along with several other men, head for the horse corral.

At the same time, some of the older men in the village were pointing to the south. Crooked Nose looked in that direction. He saw several specks on the horizon. Some people were heading toward the Sioux encampment. Crooked Nose knew that it could be more members of the tribe, but he also knew that it could be their enemies—the Crows or the Shoshones. His father and the other warriors were headed out to see if they needed to sound the alarm that would spur the entire encampment to prepare for battle.

"I can't wrestle with you now," Crooked Nose told his cousins. "I have to find out if we are going to be attacked."

That sobered his cousins. If an attack was imminent, each one of them had a responsibility. As they headed toward their own families' tipis, Crooked Nose said in a serious tone, "I will come back and tell you what I find out!" With that, he ran toward the pony corral.

Crooked Nose, like every Sioux boy when he was old enough, had been given a pony by his father and then taught to ride. Crooked Nose had already learned the techniques of fighting while riding his pony. He could cling to one side, hanging on to a strap around the pony's belly so he could shoot an arrow from under its neck without the enemy's seeing him.

When Crooked Nose reached the corral, he got his pony and headed in the direction his father and the other men had gone. Crooked Nose was sure that they weren't overly concerned about the arriving group, but they had to get ready for battle just in case it was the enemy.

When he was born, Crooked Nose's nose wasn't shaped the same way that other babies' noses were. It was bent slightly to the left. Sioux babies were often given names based on their physical appearance. When his parents named him Crooked Nose, they were only doing what the Sioux normally did. It was really a term of affection. Later in life Crooked Nose would receive his formal name, after he had a mystical experience or performed an act of bravery.

Crooked Nose quickly slapped the flank of his pony. If the people headed toward the encampment were indeed their enemies, this might be his chance to act bravely. When he saw the danger signal from the warriors ahead of him, he could rush back and warn the encampment, giving them much-needed time to prepare for the attack.

Suddenly Crooked Nose saw his father raise his hand, not for danger, but in greeting. The group was another band of Sioux headed for the encampment. Crooked Nose slapped his pony's flank, urging him on toward his relatives. He wanted to see who they were. He hoped that among them would be some more cousins his own age. They could exchange stories of what they had done during the past year. Crooked Nose wondered if any of them had received new names or had had their mystical experiences.

Finally Crooked Nose got close enough to see that it was another band of Oglalas. His father was now riding back toward the camp beside his uncle, Crazy Horse, whose name in the Sioux language—Tasunke Witko—meant holy, mystical, and inspired horse. Crazy Horse

was an Oglala holy man, a dreamer and a prophet who was respected for his wisdom and his good advice.

Crooked Nose maneuvered his pony so that he was riding directly behind his father and Crazy Horse. He nodded to Laughing One, Crazy Horse's daughter. She and her mother were walking behind one of the travois, a sledlike platform supported by two long trailing poles, the ends of which were fastened to a horse. Crooked Nose could easily tell that Laughing One's mother would soon bear a child. The thought excited him. Bear Butte was a good place to be born, he knew. The valleys and the deep woods were full of game. The rivers were cold and clear and full of fish. It was a perfect place that only Wakan Tanka, the Great Spirit, could have made for the Sioux. To be born there, Crooked Nose knew, would mean that you were very special.

"We are here, and now the child can come,"

Crazy Horse said to Two Bows. "Wakan Tanka wanted him to be born in the Black Hills."

Two Bows nodded. "If the child is a boy, then he will certainly be a great warrior," he said.

"It will be a boy," Crazy Horse told him. "It came to me in a dream, so it is to be."

Crooked Nose knew his uncle spoke the truth. A Sioux holy man always knew what dreams and visions meant.

Crooked Nose looked back at Laughing One. She was smiling at him now. It wouldn't hurt to talk to her, he decided. Even though he was now at the age when boys no longer played with girls, there was nothing wrong with remembering past summers before Laughing One started to learn what women did. They could talk about when they swam together in the cold streams and hunted small animals with bows and arrows.

"It is good to see you, Cousin," Crooked Nose said.

"It is good to see you as well," Laughing One said.

"Soon we will have a new brother," Crooked Nose said.

"Yes," Laughing One said. She blushed and then turned away from him. After that, she said very little else.

Crooked Nose wondered why he was having such a difficult time talking to Laughing One. He also didn't remember her ever looking as pretty as she did now.

He is not the boy I remember, Laughing One thought, stealing a glance at Crooked Nose, when he had turned away. She suddenly wondered how many other things at the encampment had changed since the year before.

Once in a while Crooked Nose would look back at her and smile, but he said nothing else until they reached the first tipis at the edge of the encampment.

"I shall come see my brother when he is born," Crooked Nose said.

"I shall show him to you," Laughing One said.

Two Bows waved farewell, then he and Crooked Nose rode off toward the horse corral.

Since it was customary for a family to set up its tipi among the wife's relatives, Laughing One knew they would go straight to the Brulés. The Sioux encampment was always laid out in the same way, so it would be easy to find her mother's people. They would have to wait before going to the Oglala tipis to see her father's family. She didn't know why, exactly, but she was looking forward to seeing Crooked Nose again.

When Crazy Horse's small band finally reached the Brulés, there was only the raising of hands in recognition. The visiting would have to wait until the all the tipis had been set up. This would take most of the rest of the day.

Since setting up a tipi was women's work, Laughing One immediately took over. Normally her mother would be in charge, but it was almost time for the child to be born, and Laughing One didn't want her mother lifting anything heavy. Still, her mother helped as much as she could. Having a child was a natural thing, not an illness, and so no one would ever think to tell her that she didn't have to do anything.

Although it wasn't really necessary to tell the other women what to do first, since they had done this so often, Laughing One wanted to make sure that everything went as smoothly as possible, and that no one was tempted to stop and visit before all of the tents were erected. Everything needed to be ready—and to be ready very soon—so her mother could give birth to her brother in the proper Sioux way.

"It is time to remove all the packs from the travois," Laughing One told the other women and girls.

They began doing as Laughing One instructed. Soon each family's belongings, wrapped in buffalo hide and tied securely with rope made of sinew, marked what would be the center of their tipi.

"Now we must untie the poles of the travois," Laughing One continued.

When the poles were disassembled, the women quickly set up the frames for the tipis. After that, they wrapped the painted buffalo hides around the poles.

The tipis were nearly twenty feet across at the base and almost eighteen feet high. In the winter, with a fire in the center, they would keep the families warm. In the summer the sides could be rolled up to let in the cool breezes.

When their work was finally finished, Laughing One stepped back and surveyed the job. It was good. She hoped her mother would be pleased.

Now the fires had to be lit, and each

woman, with her daughters, set about doing that. Soon the smoke was curling up through the smoke holes in the tops of the tipis and mingling with the haze that hung above the encampment.

Laughing One unrolled one of the larger buffalo blankets and helped her mother lie down. Just as the fire began to crackle to life, Laughing One noticed her mother clutch her stomach and wince in pain. Laughing One knew that the time had come for her brother to be born.

Quickly she shooed her father out of the tipi. Sioux men had no role in the birth of Sioux children. She ran to get Singing Voice and Holy Star to help deliver the baby. In their band they were the most experienced in such things. She told Black Blanket to crush berries and to fill a buffalo bladder with their juice. According to Sioux custom, a mother's milk would not be pure enough for a few days, so this would be her brother's first meal.

With birthing skills passed down from generation to generation, the child was soon delivered, and it was a boy, as Crazy Horse had said it would be.

"He has so much hair, but it's not dark like ours," Laughing One said. "It's light brown and so fine that it looks like gossamer," she added, thinking of the fine strands of cobwebs she had often seen floating in the air or caught on bushes or grass.

The women all nodded their agreement.

"I have never seen a Sioux with hair like this," Singing Voice whispered.

"And his skin, it's different too," Laughing One said almost reverently, "not like the whites who travel across our land, but lighter than that of any Sioux."

Again the women nodded.

"He is different, because he is special," Laughing One's mother said softly, "and he is special, because he was born in this special place."

"He will be a great chief," Black Blanket said.

"He will do things that no other Sioux chief has done," Holy Star said.

Laughing One knew they weren't just saying these things. They actually believed them.

Just then the baby started to cry, but instantly Laughing One's mother pinched the baby's nose between her thumb and her forefinger and, with her palm held gently against his mouth, stopped the crying. This was one of the first, and most important, things that a Sioux baby learned: No one, not even a baby, was allowed to put the tribe in danger. A single cry could guide the Crows or the Shoshones to their encampment, or even scare off buffalo during a hunt.

After her mother was comfortable and the women were gone, Laughing One sat alone by the fire and thought about what the next few years would bring to her brother. There would come a time when he would put on war paint, gather his bow and arrows, and ride with Crazy Horse out onto the plains. Laughing One and her mother would sit and do their beadwork and wonder if this time no one would come back.

Curly

By August 1844 Laughing One's mother was dead, and Crazy Horse had married Gathers Her Berries.

Laughing One's new stepmother was kind, but she wasn't very strong physically. Since Gathers Her Berries would soon have a child, Laughing One made sure she helped out with all the chores, even more than she was normally expected to do. Without being asked, she also took over most of the responsibilities for watching over her baby brother. He was almost three years old now, and everyone in the band called him "Curly."

Laughing One never failed to be amazed by Curly. She, along with the other members of their band, seemed in awe of him, partly because of Curly's light skin and curly hair, but mostly because Curly seemed to understand things that most children his age didn't.

On this day, as Laughing One sat outside their tipi doing beadwork with her friend Pretty Plume, Curly was playing on the ground with some of the other children. His hands and knees were covered with dirt. Laughing One thought Curly was playing too near a fire where some of the women were preparing the evening meal, but she didn't say anything to him. All Sioux children were free to learn in the Sioux way—by experience.

"How did you hear that Crooked Nose had a vision?" Pretty Plume asked Laughing One, continuing their conversation.

Laughing One turned away from watching

Curly. "Kills-in-Woods told me," she replied. "He saw Crooked Nose and some of his relatives at the white man's trading post on the Laramie River."

"They should not spend so much time hanging around the white man," Pretty Plume said angrily. After a couple of minutes, in a much softer voice, she said, "Do you like him, Laughing One?"

Laughing One wasn't exactly sure how she felt about Crooked Nose, but before she could say anything, she heard a soft whimpering sound. Turning quickly, she saw Curly at the edge of the fire. He was looking at the palms of his hands. The women who were cooking were busy talking to one another. They had not seen what had just happened.

Laughing One knew right away, though. Curly had thought the fire looked interesting, so he had reached into the flames and burned his hands.

Quickly Laughing One jumped up. "Get

the buffalo grease for me, Pretty Plume," she said as calmly as possible.

Laughing One rushed over to the fire, grabbed Curly around the waist, and lifted him up onto her hip. As she headed toward the tipi, she carefully avoided touching his hands, which were already turning red.

"I know it hurts, little brother, but today you have learned that fire is both our friend and our enemy," Laughing One whispered gently to Curly. "It warms us when we are cold, and it cooks our food so we can eat, but it will not allow us to get too close to it."

Inside the tipi Laughing One took the buffalo grease from Pretty Plume and immediately rubbed it on Curly's palms. When she finished, she handed him to Gathers Her Berries, who rocked him to sleep.

The next morning Curly's palms were no longer red, and Laughing One once again sang praises to Wakan Tanka, the Great Spirit, who had given them such an animal as the buffalo that supplied almost all their needs.

Their father, Crazy Horse, loved Curly. He took Curly on long walks in the open plains. Back in their tipi at night, Crazy Horse would talk to Curly about the things they had seen during their walks. "Remember the prairie dogs in their warrens?" Crazy Horse would say. "Remember the silent wings of the eagle drifting high above our heads?"

Before Curly went to sleep at night, Crazy Horse would tell Curly about a dream he had had the night before.

Laughing One, sitting on the other side of the tipi with Gathers Her Berries, rubbing buffalo fat into buffalo hide to make it soft and supple, could tell by the firelight that her father was looking at Curly's face, hoping that his son would help him explain the dream's meaning. Such was the feeling of the members of the band for Curly, that even a holy

man like Crazy Horse looked to him for answers.

A week later Curly was sitting just outside the tipi. He was watching all the activity of the camp, but he was mostly thinking about what had happened to him when he touched the flames of the cooking fire. He thought he should have been able to keep his hands there without the fire's hurting him. Curly didn't think he should fear anything.

Suddenly Curly saw Little Eagle, one of the young braves who guarded the band's horses, running toward the camp.

"The Crows are coming!" Little Eagle shouted. "The Crows are coming!"

Something inside Curly stirred. It was a feeling he had never had before. He sensed that the band was in danger, and that he should do something to help save everyone, but he was confused as to what it would be.

All over the camp, men started running

out of the tipis, some still pulling on their buckskin shirts. They carried their bows and rawhide quivers. The women quickly abandoned the cooking fires and began scooping up children and carrying them to the nearest tipi.

Just then Crazy Horse rushed out of Curly's tipi. He, too, had his bow and quiver with him.

"Father! Father!" Curly cried. "Where are you going?"

"Our old enemies have come to do us harm, my son," Crazy Horse replied. "We must stop them before they steal our horses and our mothers and daughters."

Curly stretched out his arms to Crazy Horse. "Take me with you, Father!" he said.

"You are not ready yet, my son," Crazy Horse said gently, "but that time will come soon enough."

Laughing One appeared at their father's side and quickly picked up Curly.

Curly fought her furiously. He kicked her legs with his feet and beat his hands against her arms, trying to free himself, but Laughing One held him tightly and took him inside the tipi.

Crazy Horse closed the flaps behind them. Now they were in almost total darkness, with only the embers from the fire for light.

Laughing One heard Gathers Her Berries groaning on the opposite side of the tipi. She hoped the new baby wouldn't come during the raid.

Gathers Her Berries had awakened during the night, complaining of stomach pains. Laughing One had helped Crazy Horse prepare an herbal drink for her. It seemed to ease the pain somewhat, Laughing One thought, but now Gathers Her Berries had a very high fever and lay motionless on her buffalo blanket.

Laughing One set Curly down on his own buffalo blanket. "You must be very quiet," she whispered to him. "Our stepmother needs me."

Curly watched as his sister knelt next to their stepmother, lifted her head gently, and dripped water from a gourd into her mouth.

Outside the tipi, above the crying of the other children and the wailing of the women, Curly could hear the war whoops of the Sioux warriors. Suddenly Curly let out a loud whoop of his own.

"Hush, Curly," Laughing One scolded. "Gathers Her Berries is very ill."

Curly stood up. When Laughing One turned back to Gathers Her Berries, Curly darted for the opening flap of the tipi. In seconds he was outside.

Curly heard Laughing One shouting for him to return, but he paid no attention to her. He was fascinated by what he saw in front of him. Everywhere he looked, people were running, so Curly started to run too, zigzagging his way among the tipis.

Once, a women he recognized as She

Laughs stuck her head through the opening of a tipi and said, "Curly! Come here! The Crows will get you if you don't!"

Curly ignored her and continued to weave his way through the camp. Suddenly he stopped. Ahead, at the edge of the camp, he saw the band's warriors. Although their backs were to him, he recognized his father's shirt.

"Father!" he called.

Crazy Horse didn't turn around. Curly knew that with all the other noise, his father was probably too far away to hear him. He ran closer. But when he heard several loud cracks in the distance, he stopped again. Rifles made those sounds, Curly knew. He had seen the white man's rifles before, both when they were at the trading posts and when the army scouts passed close to their village. The Sioux didn't have rifles, but Curly had heard the men in the village talking about the Indians tribes that did.

Curly thought he could hear other, more

distant war whoops. He looked beyond his father to the top of a nearby ridge. He had to squint to see clearly, but there were several men on horses. They wore feathers and their faces were painted. They were waving their rifles up and down.

These must be Crows, Curly thought. *They are not Sioux warriors.*

Curly lifted his leg to start running again toward Crazy Horse, but someone grabbed him around his waist, picked him up, and squeezed him tightly.

It was Laughing One. She had a scowl on her face.

"The Crows steal little Sioux boys, too, Curly," Laughing One said. "You must never do this again until our father has taught you what you need to know to be a warrior."

Quickly Laughing One ran back to their tipi. Curly could feel her legs as they pounded the ground. He had no idea that his sister could run so fast.

Finally they reached their tipi. Laughing One opened it quickly, pushed Curly inside, and then she followed. This time, though, she sat with her back to the entrance, so Curly could not escape again.

For just a few minutes Curly stared angrily at his sister, but when she only stared back, he decided to laugh. That made Laughing One laugh too.

On the other side of the tipi, Gathers Her Berries said in a weak voice, "Curly, come sit by me."

Curly walked over to his stepmother, lay down, and rested his head on her shoulder.

Gathers Her Berries gently stroked his hair. "Someday soon, you will be the greatest of all Sioux warriors," she told him softly.

The Special Bow

Curly now had a new brother whose name was Little Hawk. Little Hawk spent all his time with Gathers Her Berries and Laughing One, but Curly knew that it wouldn't be long before Little Hawk would want to do the same things that Curly did, and Curly would be ready to teach him.

Curly was no longer interested in the games he used to play in the dirt outside their tipi. Now, every chance he got, he watched the older boys as they practiced shooting their bows and arrows.

One game in particular fascinated Curly. The young braves would cut a hole in the center of a huge cactus lobe, and one of them would hold the cactus over his head. The other boys, armed with their bows and blunted arrows, would chase the boy all around the camp, shooting arrows at the cactus, trying to send one through the hole.

The boy holding the cactus would try to make it as difficult for the other boys as possible. That usually meant that arrow after arrow would strike every part of his body. Once in a while one of the arrows would make it through the hole, but most of the arrows missed the cactus completely.

Curly was sure that he could put an arrow through the hole in the cactus each time he shot one. Of course, he knew he'd first have to get his father to make him a bow and some arrows.

In the tipi that night, after his father had told him a story about the great deeds of

Wakan Tanka, Curly said, "I would like to have a bow and some arrows like the other boys."

"You are only six years old, Curly. You're too young. It takes great strength to pull back the bow string," Crazy Horse said. "I will make you a bow and some arrows when you are older."

"When will that be?" Curly asked.

"Soon," Crazy Horse said.

"Tomorrow?" Curly said.

"If you are strong enough tomorrow, yes," Crazy Horse said. "If you are not, no."

Curly smiled at his father. "I will be strong enough tomorrow," he said.

Crazy Horse smiled back at him. So did Laughing One and Gathers Her Berries.

Curly had seen them do that before. His family didn't think he would be ready, but he had a plan to make sure he was.

The next morning, after he had eaten his buffalo meat and berries, Curly left the tipi and headed toward the field where he knew the boys would be playing the cactus game with their bows and arrows.

Whichever boy had the cactus lobe on his head would always leave his bow on the ground, while the other boys chased him. Curly picked up the boy's bow, held it in the same way he had seen others hold their bows, and tried to pull the bow string toward him. It hardly moved. Curly couldn't believe how difficult it was. There was no way he was going to quit, though. He knew he could do it.

Each time Curly pulled on the string, he was able to move it a little closer to his body. He switched arms, thinking that one arm might work better than the other one, but that wasn't so. Soon both his arms hurt.

When the boy who had the cactus on his head returned to get his bow, Curly handed it to him.

"I'll hold your bow for you," Curly said to the new boy who now had the cactus lobe on his head.

"Thanks, Curly," the boy said. "One of these days you'll have a bow too, and you can play with us."

When the boys were out of sight, Curly started practicing with the new bow.

Curly stayed with the young braves until almost sunset. Although his arms hurt a lot, Curly didn't care, because he could now draw the bowstring almost to his chest.

When Curly got to his tipi, he sat down with his family for the evening meal, but he was too excited to eat very much.

When everyone else had finished, Curly said, "May I have a bow, Father?"

"You're too young, Curly. It takes great strength to pull the string of a bow," Crazy Horse said. "I will make you one when you are older."

"I am one moon older, Father," Curly replied seriously.

"One moon is not enough, Curly," Crazy Horse said. "You will need many more moons before you are ready."

"May I see your bow, please, Father?" Curly asked.

Crazy Horse gave him a puzzled look. Both Laughing One and Gathers Her Berries had stopped their work to see what would happen now.

Finally Crazy Horse said, "Of course, my son." He lifted the bow off a knot on one of the tipi poles and, without saying anything, handed it to Curly.

Crazy Horse's bow was almost twice the size of the bows the boys had been using for their games, but Curly took it anyway. He grasped the wood with his left hand and the string with his right fingers. Holding the bow as far away from his chest as he could, he slowly began to pull on the string.

For just a moment Curly didn't think he could move the string, but then he began to draw it slowly toward him. He was sure he heard Laughing One and Gathers Her Berries gasp. He could feel his father's eyes on him. He wondered if they were wide with surprise.

Finally Curly had pulled the string as close to his chest as he could. He let it go and it twanged loudly. The release almost caused him to drop the bow, but he managed to hold on.

Slowly Curly turned to face his father. "May I have my own bow now?" he asked.

Crazy Horse smiled at him. "Yes, my son," he said. "Tomorrow you and I will look for a special tree from which to make your bow."

Curly hardly slept that night. The next morning no one said anything about what had happened the night before, and for a while Curly thought his father had forgotten.

Finally Crazy Horse said, "We shall go now, Curly. We will spend the day finding just the right sapling out of which to make your first bow."

Curly's heart started to pound. "I am ready, Father," he said.

Crazy Horse picked up his ax, and he and Curly headed toward a small creek that flowed into the Powder River.

When they reached it, Curly said, "There are many trees here, Father. We can make lots of bows from them."

Crazy Horse shook his head. "There is one special tree that Wakan Tanka grew just for your bow, Curly," he said. "We must look until we find it."

Curly started to ask his father how they would recognize it, but he suddenly realized that the tree itself would tell them, if they only paid attention to it in the Sioux way. Curly would do that.

For a while they looked at the trees on their side of the creek, but none of them seemed right. Crazy Horse would grab the trunks, pull them toward him, and then let them go, testing to see how fast they sprang back into shape.

Finally Curly said, "I don't think my tree is on this side of the creek, Father."

Crazy Horse nodded. He took Curly's hand, and together they waded across the creek.

Once they were on the opposite bank, Curly ran from tree to tree. From time to time he stopped and put his ear against the trunk, hoping that the sapling would speak to him, but nothing happened until he reached one particular tree that was almost in the middle of a stand. Curly thought there was something special about this tree. He reached out and touched it. It even felt different. He couldn't take his eyes off it.

"Father!" Curly called. "Here is my tree."

Crazy Horse came up from behind him. "It is an ash sapling, Son. I was hoping to find one just like this."

Crazy Horse grabbed the trunk and pulled it toward him. When he let it go, the trunk sprang back immediately to its original shape. "You are right, Curly," he said. "This is the one."

Crazy Horse started hacking at the base of the trunk with his ax.

Curly watched as chips of wood flew out with every strike. He could smell the sweet sap, and he knew it would be a smell he would always remember.

Finally the ax blade cut all the way through the trunk, and with a swishing sound the sapling fell to the ground.

Crazy Horse quickly lopped off the branches. He saved the smaller ones to use for arrows.

When he finished, he handed the ax to Curly.

Curly had watched his father carry the ax, so he grasped the wooden handle, just under the blade, and held it a few inches away from his side. It was much heavier than it looked, but Curly was pleased that his father would trust him to carry it.

Crazy Horse smiled at him, then he lifted the sapling trunk onto his shoulder.

"We'll take this back to our camp," Crazy Horse said. "We'll start making your bow right away."

"Thank you, Father," Curly said.

With Crazy Horse in the lead, they recrossed the creek and headed back to the camp.

Gathers Her Berries, Laughing One, and Little Hawk were waiting for them outside the tipi.

"We found my tree," Curly said to them. "It was waiting for us, just like Father said it would be."

Crazy Horse gently set the sapling on the ground. With his ax, he cut it in half.

"Why did you do that?" Curly asked.

"Your bow is already inside the tree, Curly," Crazy Horse replied. "We just have to find it." He laid down the ax. "Come here. Let me show you."

Curly looked closely at the two halves of the sapling. His father was right. They didn't look the same. He thought he could actually see the shape of a bow inside one of the halves.

"Which one is it, Curly?" Crazy Horse asked.

Curly pointed.

Crazy Horse nodded. "We have to take out the bow carefully," he said. "We will begin now, but it won't be ready to come out for several moons."

Crazy Horse picked up the half of the sapling Curly had indicated, and, with Curly behind him, went into the tipi and sat cross-legged by the fire.

Curly watched as his father began to pare away the bark of the trunk.

"It is very important that the wood dry evenly, Curly," Crazy Horse said. "Removing all the bark will help it do that."

When the bark was all off, Crazy Horse began turning the wood over and over in his hands. "Now I need to find the middle," he said. He stood up and balanced the piece of wood on one finger, moving it ever so slightly to find the perfect center. "This is important, Curly," he added. "The true center of the sapling is where the grip of the bow is carved."

Over the next two weeks Crazy Horse, always with Curly by his side, worked on the wood with his steel-bladed knife which he had gotten at the white man's trading post on the Laramie River. When he was finished he would leave the piece of wood by the fire, but not too close, so that it would continue to dry.

Curly watched in amazement as his bow slowly started to take shape. Finally it was finished.

Crazy Horse handed the bow to Curly. Curly wrapped his hand around the grip. It fit perfectly.

"Your bow should be part of your body, Son," Crazy Horse said. "It will breathe when you breathe."

Curly nodded. He believed that.

Crazy Horse got a small brush made from horsehair and three small gourds that contained colored paint made from berries and other plants. He took the bow from Curly. Using the brush, Crazy Horse painted several designs on the bow. When he finished, he wrapped the grip in deer hide.

"We'll put your bow by the fire again tonight, so that it can dry one more time," Crazy Horse said, "but tomorrow, I will attach a string of sinew, and it will be ready so you can join the other boys in their games."

Curly yawned. "Thank you, Father," he said sleepily. He was too tired to tell him that he was no longer interested in playing games with the other boys. Now he wanted to use his bow to hunt buffalo.

The Magic Deer

When Curly was nine, he started spending more time with an older boy named Hump. Hump got his name, just like all Sioux children, from his physical appearance. His back was deformed.

At first Hump bragged a lot about what a great warrior he would be one day, but slowly, as Hump realized that Curly didn't need to be impressed, that he just wanted Hump to be his friend, he stopped. Soon Curly and Hump became inseparable. They were *kolas*.

As the months passed, they wandered farther and farther away from their camp. They seemed to draw strength from each other. Together they did things that neither one of them would likely have done separately. They were like two halves of the same person. Even though they had fun, they knew what they were doing was serious. They knew the life of a Sioux warrior was harsh and unforgiving. If they were unprepared, they would die in battle. If they were prepared, they would be honored by their tribe.

Curly now had his fourth bow. It was larger and more intricately decorated than the first one his father had made for him. Curly himself had killed the otter whose skin was used for the quivers that held his and Hump's arrows.

One morning in late summer, Hump came to the door of Curly's tipi and called to him.

Curly appeared, wiping away some blackberry juice from his mouth. He grinned at his friend. Curly could tell by the sparkle in Hump's eyes that he had something exciting to tell him.

"I saw a deer's tracks at the creek this morning," Hump said.

"Are they fresh?" Curly asked.

Hump nodded. "I followed them a short way. I'm sure it's headed for the Paha Sapa." Hump nodded to the nearby peaks of the Black Hills, as though Curly wouldn't understand what he was talking about.

Curly and Hump had hunted only small game before. Although rabbits made a good stew, they were nothing compared to venison. If he and Hump could bring back a deer, their families would be even more proud of how they were becoming great hunters.

Curly grabbed his bow and quiver. He said nothing to the rest of his family, and they didn't question him. He was no longer a child, and his family knew they could trust him.

Hump led the way to the creek bank where he had seen the deer tracks.

Curly knelt down and looked at them. "It's a huge buck, Hump," he said excitedly. "I think he made these tracks right before you were here." He stood up. "If we hurry, we can catch up with him."

Quickly, but stealthily, Curly and Hump followed the tracks through the woods. Curly could tell by the spacing of the hoof marks that the buck was neither frightened nor in a hurry. It was as if the deer knew it was being followed and wanted the challenge.

When the creek turned, the buck's tracks left its banks and started uphill on rockier ground. Now the tracks weren't as easy to follow, but Curly and Hump prided themselves on being excellent trackers.

Higher and higher they climbed up the side of the hill. Soon they were out of the bigger stands of trees and into mostly clumps of trees standing in boulder-strewn meadows.

They had almost reached the top of one hill when Curly stopped. He grabbed Hump's arm and pulled him behind a boulder.

"What did you . . . ," Hump started to say, but Curly put a hand over his mouth. Hump's eyes flashed angrily, but he remained silent.

After a few moments Curly motioned that they should stand up slowly. Together they peered over the top of the boulder.

Hump's jaw dropped.

A large buck stood just at the edge of a clump of trees, almost blending in with the bark of the trunks.

"I have never seen a rack of antlers that big," Curly whispered. "This is surely the biggest deer in the world."

Hump nodded his agreement.

Suddenly the buck's ears twitched, and Curly pulled Hump back down behind the boulder.

"Stop doing that," Hump hissed at Curly. He slowly began to stand up.

Curly did the same.

When their eyes reached the top of the boulder again, they were stunned to see the buck looking straight at them.

"He can see us," Curly said. "He knows we're here."

Suddenly the buck stepped out far enough away from the trees that the sunlight illuminated its head. Its huge eyes seemed to be full of fire. The sunlight reflecting off its antlers looked like streaks of lightning.

"We need to get a little closer," Hump said. "I think we're too far away to shoot him from here."

"We can't shoot him," Curly said. He hadn't taken his eyes off the buck.

"That's why we came, Curly," Hump said. He looked at Curly. "Are you afraid of him?"

Curly felt the anger rising inside him. How could Hump even think such a thing? he wondered. "I am not afraid of anything," Curly whispered.

Hump squatted back down on the ground and started slowly crawling on his stomach out from behind the boulder. This time Curly didn't try to stop him.

When Hump was just a few feet away from the boulder, Curly peeked over the top to see if the buck had noticed. The deer seemed to be watching Hump, but it didn't act frightened by what was happening. Curly knew that he couldn't stay where he was. He decided to follow Hump. For some reason Curly himself didn't yet understand, he had decided that they shouldn't kill the deer.

Curly got down on his stomach and started crawling through the tall grass after Hump. Soon he was right behind him. As they headed toward another group of trees, Hump silently withdrew three arrows from his quiver and grasped them tightly in his right hand. The best Sioux warriors could sometimes shoot up to six arrows so fast that the last one would already be heading toward the target before the first one hit, but Curly knew that Hump wasn't that good yet. He wondered why Hump hadn't left his arrows in his quiver. Of course, Curly knew that Hump sometimes liked to pretend he was already a great Sioux warrior.

Suddenly Hump stopped. "I'm sure I can kill it from here," he whispered. He dropped two of the arrows and fitted the third one to his bow string.

Curly laid his hand on Hump's arm. Shaking his head, he said, "No, Hump, this deer is *wakan.*"

"You are wrong, Curly. This deer is not holy," Hump said. "It is just a deer."

Curly shook his head again.

"If he is *wakan,* then my arrow will not harm him," Hump argued. "If it is just a regular deer, then tonight, our families will feast on its meat."

Curly knew that Hump would not listen to him. Now it was a matter of pride that he slay the buck.

Out of the corner of one eye, Curly saw Hump's bow rise as he prepared to shoot the arrow. Suddenly the string snapped, and the arrow shot toward the buck.

Curly couldn't believe what he was seeing. The buck just stood there and watched as the arrow approached. It made no attempt whatsoever to move.

Seconds later a sound like a crack of thunder echoed in the meadow as the arrow struck the buck's huge antlers. The buck still didn't move. It just stood where it was, staring at Curly and Hump.

Curly hoped now that Hump would believe that the deer was holy, but instead, without saying a word, Hump notched another arrow and let it fly toward the buck. This one also missed its mark and landed in the soft ground to the right of the animal. Still the buck didn't move.

Angrily Hump notched a third arrow, pulled back the bowstring, and sent it racing toward the animal. This time the arrow fell to the buck's left side.

"He is truly *wakan,* Hump," Curly said. "Your arrows would have found him if he weren't."

"What you want my ears to hear, Curly, is not what you are thinking inside," Hump said angrily. He stood up. In a louder voice, he added, "Inside, you are thinking that I will never make a great Sioux warrior!"

"No, Hump, that is not what I was thinking," Curly insisted. "You are my *kola,* one true friend, and I would never think that of you."

Suddenly the buck snorted, pawed the earth, and began charging toward Curly and Hump.

Hump looked up, saw the buck coming toward them, and notched another arrow. Without thinking, Curly notched an arrow too. Hump's arrow flew toward the charging buck. Once again it missed. Hump stood where he was, in the path of the charging animal, and notched another arrow, but Curly pulled back his bow string and let his arrow fly. Curly's arrow struck the buck in its chest and plunged so deep that only the end feathers were showing. The buck stopped suddenly in midstride, as though it were suspended in air, and then, with a loud thud, fell to the earth.

Hump blinked unbelievingly, then turned to Curly. "Why did you do that?" he screamed. "Why did you shoot my deer?"

"He would have killed you if I had not shot him, Hump," Curly said, stunned at his friend's anger. "He was headed straight toward you, and your arrows kept missing him."

"You didn't give me a chance to shoot my last arrow," Hump insisted. "It would have killed the deer, just like yours did."

Curly had never seen Hump act this way before. He didn't know what to say.

"This is my deer!" Hump shouted.

"Yes, it is your deer," Curly said. "Take it. I don't want it."

"I don't want it either," Hump said. He turned and started back down the hill.

"We can't leave the deer here!" Curly shouted to him. "Wakan Tanka will be angry with us!"

Hump said nothing. Instead he broke into a trot and continued down the hill.

"Hump!" Curly shouted.

For the first time in his life, Curly was uncertain what to do. He looked at the huge buck that lay still just a few feet from him. There was no way he could carry it back to the camp by himself. He thought about carving out some of the meat, in the way that he had seen his father and the other men do, but he knew it would be such a small amount that it would barely feed his family for one meal. What, then, would happen to the rest of the deer? Wakan Tanka had given the deer to the Sioux to help feed and clothe them. He would be angry if Curly did not do the right thing. Curly suddenly realized that even if Hump had not stalked off in anger, the two of them would not have been able to carry the huge animal back to the camp. Feeling a little better, he set off in search of Hump, but Hump was no longer in sight. Curly called to him several times, but in the echos that came back to him, he heard only his voice, never that of Hump.

Finally Curly arrived back at his village. Not seeing Hump anywhere, he went straight to his tipi. When he entered, he said nothing to anyone. Instead he lay down on his buffalo blanket and watched the smoke from the cook fire as it curled up toward the hole at the top of the tipi.

After a few minutes Crazy Horse came over and sat down next to him. "What has happened, Curly, to change the happiness I saw this morning to the sadness I see now?" he asked.

"Nothing," Curly replied.

When Crazy Horse said no more, but continued to stay where he was, Curly sat up slowly. He told Crazy Horse everything that had happened.

"Why did you think the deer was holy?" Crazy Horse asked him.

Curly told him about the deer's eyes and about the sound of thunder that the deer's antlers had made.

Crazy Horse stood. He held out his hand to Curly and said, "I want you to take me to the spot where you shot this deer."

Together Crazy Horse and Curly retraced the path that Curly and Hump had taken earlier that day. When they reached the spot where the deer had fallen, there was nothing there.

"Someone has come for it," Curly exclaimed.

Crazy Horse knelt on the ground. "There is no blood here, Curly," he said.

"Is my father saying that I am not telling the truth about the deer?" Curly asked angrily.

Crazy Horse stood up. Calmly he said, "No, my son. I know you would never make up something like this. What it tells me is that the deer really was holy, just as you thought, but it also needed to be a regular deer for Hump."

"I don't understand," Curly said.

"Hump still needs to prove to himself that he can be a great Sioux warrior, so he wanted to kill a real deer," Crazy Horse said. "In your heart you know that you no longer need to do that."

Now Curly was more confused than ever. "Are you saying that if Hump hadn't left, the deer would still be here?"

Crazy Horse nodded. "Wakan Tanka has many faces, Curly," he said. "He puts on whichever face a Sioux needs to see. To Hump, he was a regular deer, because that's what Hump needed. To you, it was something else. If

Hump had stayed, there would be deer meat for our band, and together, the two of you, as *kolas,* would have slain a deer. But when Hump left, Wakan Tanka knew that you didn't need to prove yourself, so that's why there is nothing here."

Curly thought for a minute. "What was Wakan Tanka to me?" he asked.

"Time will tell," Crazy Horse said. "You must continue to keep your eyes and ears and your mind open and listen to what Wakan Tanka tells you." He patted Curly's head. "You are very special to me, Son, but you are even more special to Wakan Tanka."

"What about Hump?" Curly said. "He's my best friend, yet he is angry at me now."

"Hump is still learning that Sioux warriors must always hunt and fight together as a group, not as individuals, if they are to be successful. He will not stay angry with you long, Curly," Crazy Horse said. "You are his *kola,* and he is your *kola.*"

Curly understood. He and Hump really were special friends. Special friends might have arguments from time to time, but nothing could keep them apart forever.

The Raid on Conquering Bear's Camp

In the summer of 1851, when Curly was almost ten, he, Little Hawk, and Hump were one day's ride from their camp when they spotted a long wagon train of white settlers. It was slowly making its way northwest along what the Sioux now called the "Holy Road" because the trail had become so important to the Americans.

The Sioux believed that they had the right to take anything they wanted from anyone who invaded their sacred hunting grounds, so Curly, Little Hawk, and Hump hid behind some large boulders to watch the wagon train and to decide whether or not to raid it.

For years, Curly knew, this trail had been used only by the Indians of the plains. But right before he was born, some of the Sioux, in friendship, had showed the white settlers the easiest way through the Rocky Mountains as they headed toward a land the Americans called "Oregon."

Soon thousands of settlers were traveling this road, which they now called the "Oregon Trail." They killed the buffalo for no reason at all and left their broken wagons and garbage everywhere. Too late the Sioux realized they had made a mistake in befriending the white people.

"There are no soldiers around, Curly," Hump said. "Let's ride down and see what we can get to take back to our village."

Little Hawk looked expectantly at his brother. "We could get some nice things for Mother and Sister," he said.

Curly shook his head.

"Why not?" Hump asked. "Are you afraid of the white man now?"

"No, but Colonel Kearny said that his soldiers would punish us if we raided the wagon trains, Hump," Curly said. He looked at Little Hawk. "What the white man has isn't worth what would happen to our people."

"That never stopped us before," Hump said. "Why should it stop us now?"

Curly took a deep breath. "It's just a feeling I have, that's all," he said.

Curly could tell that some of the drivers were just young children. There could be only one reason for that, he knew. Their parents were lying ill inside the wagons. If he and Hump raided the train, they could be attacked by the white man's diseases, which were worse than any guns they could aim at you.

Curly shuddered as he remembered what had happened the previous year. He and Hump had ridden into a Sioux encampment on one of their many trips together. It was such a strange sight. There was no one walking around.

Curly and Hump called out, telling the people who they were and asking for their hospitality, for they were hungry, but no one answered them.

Slowly, cautiously, Curly and Hump dismounted, tied their ponies to one of the poles that was used for drying meat, and made their way toward the first tipi. Before they ever reached the opening, the smell made their stomachs lurch. Still, they managed to look inside, but just as fast, they backed outside, trembling at the sight that had confronted them.

It was obvious to Curly that these people had been dead for several days. He already knew what he and Hump would probably find in the other tipis, but he said, "We must see if there is anyone who is still alive."

Hump grudgingly followed Curly as he ran

from tipi to tipi. Everyone was dead, and it looked to Curly as though their last moments had been horrible.

"We have to warn the people in our camp," Curly had told Hump. He looked fearfully around him. "These unseen things that bring death to our people may already be on their way there."

Quickly Curly and Hump had mounted their ponies and headed toward their camp. On the way they stopped at several streams to wash off any of the white man's diseases they might have picked up in the dead camp.

When they had finally reached their own camp with the tale of what they had seen, Crazy Horse and some of the other warriors hurriedly had a council meeting. Within just a few hours, the entire band had packed up everything and had headed toward the Black Hills, where everyone was sure the Great Spirit would protect them. No one got sick, and by the next year the diseases seemed to have disappeared. Some said the diseases had gone to attack the enemies of the Sioux, so Curly's band moved back closer to the Laramie River.

There were now more and more white settlers on the Holy Road. There were also more and more soldiers to make sure that the Sioux, the Crows, the Cheyenne, and the Shoshones didn't bother them.

Now, just as the last wagon disappeared in the dust, some soldiers wearing their blue uniforms came into view.

"You were right, Curly," Hump said. "If we had raided the wagon train, the soldiers would have either killed us or put us in their prison."

Curly nodded. He was glad the soldiers had come along. Hump could see them. He couldn't see the white man's diseases and would not have accepted that as an excuse from Curly for not raiding the wagon train.

When the line of soldiers below them had passed, Curly and Hump mounted their horses and headed back to their camp.

When they arrived there, a white soldier, flanked by two Sioux scouts dressed in white men's clothes, was just riding in.

Curly saw his father and the other warriors walk out to the edge of the camp to meet them.

"Quick, Hump," Curly said. "We need to put our ponies in the corral and find out what the white man wants."

"I'm not interested in hearing him talk, because he will only tell lies," Hump said. "I'll put our ponies in the corral, if you want to listen, though."

"Thank you, Hump," Curly said as he dismounted and headed toward the warriors who had gathered near the three men.

"My name is David Mitchell," the white soldier said. "The president of the United States has sent me here to give you a message."

Mitchell explained that he was going from camp to camp, telling everyone the same thing. The president no longer wanted to fight the Sioux, the Cheyenne, the Shoshones, or the Crows. He wanted all the Indians of the plains to meet for a council in just two weeks at Fort Laramie, a new fort on the Laramie River. While Mitchell and the Sioux scouts waited, Crazy Horse and the other warriors and elders of the village met. Finally they agreed to the request.

After Mitchell and the scouts left, the people in Curly's band began getting ready for the trip down to Fort Laramie. Everything was packed up and put on travois. The trip took four days. As they drew close to the fort, Curly was shocked at what he saw.

"There has never been such a gathering of tribes," Crazy Horse told him and Little Hawk. "There are over ten thousand people here."

Curly looked at Fort Laramie in the distance. It was surrounded only by a wall of mud, unlike other forts, which had strong wooden stockades.

"Will there be battles, Father?" Little Hawk asked.

Crazy Horse shook his head. "No, we are here to talk about how to get along with one another."

Curly couldn't imagine how that would ever happen. What were the Sioux expected to do if the white settlers continued to cross Sioux land, killing the buffalo and bringing their diseases? How could the Sioux be expected to get along with the Crow, who had always been their enemies? Curly didn't understand the mind of the white man. Try as he might, he could not figure out how the white man thought about anything.

Still, for the next several days, Curly couldn't remember when he had ever had so much fun. He was surrounded not only by friends, but by enemies as well, and yet he didn't feel threatened. In fact, he, along with Little Hawk and Hump, played games with Shoshone boys their ages. When they introduced themselves to some Crow boys, they decided to stage mock raids on each other's camps. After the raids were over, they lay on the banks of the Laramie River and bragged to one another about their successes. They taught one another words in their languages. If they couldn't make themselves understood, then they used signs.

Maybe we can learn things from the white man after all, Curly thought one day when he was sitting next to a Crow boy, thinking not about killing him, but about the next game they would play.

That evening, when Curly started to tell Crazy Horse how he had felt that day by the river, he could tell by the look on his father's face that something was bothering him.

After the family had eaten that night, just before Curly lay down on his buffalo blanket, he said, "Are things going well, my father?"

Crazy Horse took a deep breath and let it out. "It is difficult to tell, my son," he said. "The Great White Father has promised us all the kinds of things that he says will make life better for our tribes, but we also have to promise him a great many things."

"What, Father?" Curly asked.

"The Sioux, the Cheyenne, the Shoshone, and the Crow must promise not to attack the wagon trains on the Holy Road," Crazy Horse said. "We must also promise not to attack one another."

"Who is to make this promise, Father?" Curly asked.

"Conquering Bear," Crazy Horse replied.

"I don't understand, Father," Curly said. "Conquering Bear is a great warrior, and he is a Brulé, of my mother's people, but how can he speak for you?"

"He can't, Curly, but the white men insist that only one Sioux speak for the rest of us," Crazy Horse said. "This is the white man's way."

Suddenly Curly was angry with himself. How could he have sat talking to a Crow boy on the banks of the river, when the Crows were the mortal enemies of the Sioux? What if that boy's father or older brother—or even that boy himself—had raided his village before? What if they had killed members of his tribe? How could Curly ever be friends with these people? How could the white man expect this to happen?

Without saying anything, Curly lay down, but he didn't go to sleep for a long while. His mind was still confused by what was happening around him.

Two days later Curly stood at the front of the huge throng watching a representative from each tribe, dressed in the uniform of a United States Army general, but with his face in full war paint, put a mark on a piece of paper. Curly didn't understand how a piece of paper could make the white men so happy, but it did, and that seemed to be all they wanted. As soon as each chief had signed it, the white men said the Indians were free to go back to their homes.

As Curly and his family set about taking down their tipi to put it on the travois, Crazy Horse said, "I have agreed to join our band with the band led by Man-Afraid-of-His-Horses. I think it will make us stronger."

Curly liked Man-Afraid-of-His-Horses. He knew his name meant that he was such a feared warrior that his enemies were even afraid of the horses he rode. But if the piece of paper the white man now had was meant to protect the Indians, then Curly didn't understand why his father felt the need to join up with Man-Afraid-of-His-Horses and his people.

"Is there something wrong, Father?" Curly asked. "Are we not already strong enough?"

Crazy Horse shook his head. "The piece of paper that the white men will take to the president of the United States is full of promises which cannot be kept, my son," he said. "There will be trouble soon."

Curly soon realized that his father was right. It wasn't long before everything returned to the way it had been.

Over the next two years, Curly rode with Hump, Little Hawk, and other warriors of the new band to raid wagon trains on the Holy Road. They stole not only cattle and horses, but also coffee and sugar, two things that some members of their band now considered almost as important as buffalo meat. At first the raids were easy because the white settlers believed in the paper the tribes had signed at Fort Laramie, and there were usually no soldiers with the wagon trains.

"Two of the settlers kept saying that we were violating the treaty we signed," Hump said to Curly after one raid. "Is that what that paper said, that we wouldn't raid the wagon trains?"

"We've always raided the wagon trains, Curly," Little Hawk said. "Why would the chiefs tell the white men we wouldn't do it?"

"It doesn't matter," Curly said. "The white men aren't keeping their promises either."

"What do you mean?" Hump asked.

"I'll show you," Curly said. "Follow me."

The three of them rode for several miles until they reached the edge of a bluff.

"Look down there," Curly said.

"What is that?" Little Hawk asked.

"Buffalo that the white settlers shot for no reason at all," Curly said.

"It is a waste of what the Great Spirit has given us," Hump said. "We only kill when we need the meat or the skins."

Curly nodded. "The white men always kill more than they need, and sometimes, they kill only for the fun of it."

One week later Man-Afraid-of-His-Horses decided to move his band close to Fort Laramie for the winter to be near the supplies the Indians had been promised. With all the changes coming to their land, the Sioux were finding it more and more difficult to get enough food to survive the winters. Curly knew that his father didn't think this was a good idea, but he didn't argue with Man-Afraid-of-His-Horses. The band set up its camp next to a band led by Conquering Bear. There were several other bands camped nearby, alongside the Holy Road. To Curly it was obvious the Sioux were becoming more and more dependent on the white man for their food.

When some of the band grumbled, Man-Afraid-of-His-Horses said, "We will not survive the winter without the white man's supplies."

The members of the band knew he was right, but it still angered them that their traditional way of life had changed so much.

After the camp had been set up, Curly gathered Hump and Little Hawk and said, "We are Sioux. We can still hunt in our Sioux way." With that they crossed the river and paralleled the Holy Road toward what Curly remembered as a place where buffalo always grazed. When they reached the spot, though, they found only broken wagons and piles of broken furniture. The sight made Curly sick to his stomach. It also made him angry.

As Curly, Hump, and Little Hawk headed back toward the Holy Road, they saw a wagon train on its way to Fort Laramie. At the end, there was a man whipping a lame cow that was tied to the back of his wagon.

"Come on, Curly!" Hump said.

Curly wanted more than anything to vent his anger on the settlers, but he knew that it would be a mistake. "We are too near Fort Laramie, Hump," he said. "We can't raid the wagon train."

"Well, we can pretend," Hump said.

Little Hawk grinned at Curly.

Curly smiled. "Yes, I guess we could pretend," he said.

The three of them raced their ponies

toward the wagon train, screaming as fiercely as they could. The settlers began urging the oxen to move faster. It was obvious that the settlers were frightened by what they thought was an Indian raid.

Curly, Hump, and Little Hawk whooped and hollered as they raced up and down the sides of the wagon train. Just as they passed the camp of another one of the Sioux bands, this one led by Conquering Bear, several young warriors rode out to join what they saw as a game.

Suddenly the lame cow broke loose from the wagon and started limping toward the camp.

"You heathens!" the man shouted at Curly and the other warriors. "See what you did! That's my cow!"

"You shouldn't have beaten it," Curly shouted to the man. "You white people do not know how to treat your animals!"

"You hold your tongue, you savage!" the

man shouted to Curly. "I'll have no Indian talk to me that way."

Curly saw one of the young warriors, a boy he knew as High Forehead, put an arrow in his bow and aim it at the cow. It pierced the cow's side, and the cow dropped in its tracks.

"You killed it!" the man shouted. He shook his fist at them. "That cow gave milk for my babies!"

Hump whipped his pony's flanks and started after the man. The man turned around and ran toward the wagon train, which by now had almost disappeared into the clouds of dust as it raced toward Fort Laramie.

The next day, when Curly, Hump, and Little Hawk went back to visit with the young warriors of Conquering Bear's camp, there were several soldiers there.

"Why are they here?" Curly asked a boy called Raining Face.

"The one talking is Lieutenant Fleming," Raining Face said. "He is demanding that Conquering Bear turn over High Forehead to him."

Curly started to get closer to the crowd, but Little Hawk pulled him back. "He will know we were there with High Forehead, Curly," he said. "The soldiers will take us to the fort too, and put us in their prison."

"I am not afraid of the white soldiers," Curly said.

He pulled away and walked toward the edge of the crowd.

"I cannot give you High Forehead," Conquering Bear said.

"Why can't you?" Lieutenant Fleming demanded. "Is he no longer in your camp?"

"No, he is still here, but I have no right to give him to you," Conquering Bear said. "He is a Miniconjou, and I am a Brulé."

"The Great White Father named you the chief of all the Sioux," Lieutenant Fleming insisted. "You have the right to tell any member of the Sioux tribe what to do."

"I do not have that right," Conquering Bear insisted, "but I shall be glad to give the white man any horse he wants from my corral."

"No! That is not enough," Lieutenant Fleming insisted. "The man who did this must be punished!"

"I am Brulé. High Forehead is Miniconjou," Conquering Bear repeated. "I have no right to give him to you."

"I shall return to your camp tomorrow at this time," Lieutenant Fleming said angrily. "You will hand over High Forehead to me then, or you will be sorry."

With that the soldiers rode out of the encampment.

The warriors surrounded Conquering Bear. "We will kill the white soldiers!" they shouted. "We will kill them all if they come back tomorrow."

Curly hurried back to Hump and Little Hawk. "Hump, you and I will stay here," he said. "Little Hawk, you go back to our parents and tell them that the Brulés are preparing to fight the white soldiers tomorrow."

"I want to stay, Curly," Little Hawk said. "I want to fight the white soldiers too."

Curly shook his head. "No, Little Hawk, Hump and I will not fight the soldiers. This is between the Brulés and the Miniconjous and the white soldiers. It is not between the Oglalas and the white soldiers. Hump and I will do no fighting."

Disappointed, Little Hawk headed out of the village.

Hump looked at his best friend. "Why are we staying, if we do not plan to fight?" he demanded.

Curly didn't have an answer. He just felt that he needed to be in the camp to witness the event. He was sure that soon enough he would be in battle against other white soldiers.

Curly and Hump found Raining Face and stayed close to him. As it grew late, Raining Face offered his family's tipi for Curly and Hump to spend the night. During the night Curly was awakened by movement. Raining Face's two brothers were slipping quietly out of the tipi. When Curly thought he wouldn't be noticed, he left the tipi to see where they were going. A large group of warriors was heading toward the trees at the rear of the encampment. It was all Curly could do to keep from joining them, but he kept reminding himself that this was not an Oglala fight.

Curly stayed awake for the rest of the night. Just after dawn he heard some of the women at the campfires, but he knew there wasn't really as much noise as there would usually be. When he peeked outside, he saw only a few women tending the fires. He was sure that the rest of the women and children were still inside the tipis.

Suddenly, in the distance, Curly heard the sounds of horses. Within minutes a large group of soldiers had entered the encampment. Curly was sure they were not the same soldiers who had been there the day before. Two of the horses were pulling large guns called "cannons."

Now Hump and Raining Face were awake and huddled beside Curly, looking out the entrance of the tipi.

They saw Conquering Bear come out of his tipi to meet the soldiers.

"I am Lieutenant Grattan," the lead solider said. "I have come for the man called High Forehead."

"Why do you do this?" Conquering Bear asked. "We are a peaceful people. We have offered to repay the white man more than his cow was worth."

Lieutenant Grattan turned to the two

soldiers who had been pulling the cannons. "Aim those guns at this man," he shouted.

Raining Face gasped.

Curly clenched his fists in anger. With all his heart he wanted to attack these men who would dare harm Conquering Bear.

Two older warriors walked up to stand beside Conquering Bear.

"I will only ask you once more," Lieutenant Grattan shouted. "Hand over High Forehead."

"He is over there," one of the warriors said. He pointed into the direction of another tipi.

"Send him a message," Lieutenant Grattan said to the soldiers standing by the cannons.

The men fired two rounds at High Forehead's tipi.

Suddenly hundreds of arrows rained down on the soldiers. Several of the men, including Lieutenant Grattan, were struck instantly and fell from their horses. The others panicked and started firing their rifles in every direction.

Curly and Hump eased out of the tipi and crawled on their stomachs to where they could see the Brulé warriors running from the trees toward the outmanned soldiers.

The arrows continued to rain down on the soldiers. Within minutes they all lay dead on the ground.

Curly suddenly noticed Conquering Bear lying on the ground in front of his tipi.

"Hump!" Curly shouted. "We have to help the chief!"

He started running toward Conquering Bear. Hump was right behind him. They reached the chief at the same time as some of the other warriors.

Curly could tell that Conquering Bear was still breathing, but he was bleeding from several wounds. The warriors picked him up and carried him into his tipi.

Curly stood where he was, looking at Conquering Bear's blood in the dust. He couldn't take his eyes off it. He was sure this was only the beginning of his battles with the white soldiers.

The Vision

That night Man-Afraid-of-His-Horses called all the Oglala warriors—young and old—to the center of their encampment for an important meeting.

"We must talk about what our band should do now," he said in a quiet voice. "I want to know what all of you are thinking."

To Curly, Man-Afraid-of-His-Horses no longer sounded like a great leader. He seemed confused.

"I say we ride to Fort Laramie, kill all the soldiers, and then burn the fort to the ground!" He Dog shouted. "This land is ours, and we need to take it back."

"No, no, no! We should not do that," Lone Bear shouted. "The whites are too many, and they will just send more soldiers to kill our people."

There was a murmur of agreement.

"The Great White Father will understand that the killings were not the fault of the Oglalas," Little Big Man added.

"I say we leave," Crazy Horse said, and Curly thought his father's voice sounded stronger than all the rest of the men. "We do not need the white man to give us food. We Sioux have always been able to take care of ourselves. We should go as far away from the white man as possible."

"Crazy Horse is right!" Red Feather shouted. "I never want to see another white man for the rest of my life."

For several minutes Man-Afraid-of-His-Horses was silent, then he slowly raised his hand and said, "Our holy man speaks wisely. We will do as Crazy Horse has suggested."

That night, with everyone in the band helping, the Oglala took down their tipis, gathered up the rest of their belongings, and put everything on travois. When the moon was high, they quietly left their campsite and crossed the Laramie River.

He Dog rode up to Man-Afraid-of-His-Horses. "The Brulés have broken camp too, and are starting to cross downstream," He Dog reported.

"That is good," Man-Afraid-of-His-Horses said. "I think we should ride east together with Conquering Bear's band, in case the white soldiers decide to come after us."

Crazy Horse nodded. He looked over at Curly, who was riding beside him. "We will be stronger together, and the Brulés are your mother's people. It is only right."

"Hump and I will ride downstream to tell them that's what we want to do," Curly said.

Man-Afraid-of-His-Horses nodded.

Curly found Hump riding with his family toward the end of the band. He told his friend of the plan to ride east with the Brulés.

"I've been worried about Conquering Bear," Curly said. "Now I can find out how he is. I want you to ride with me."

Together Curly and Hump paralleled the banks of the Laramie River until they reached the Brulés.

"Where is Conquering Bear?" Curly asked one of the chief's wives.

She pointed to a travois. Curly and Hump rode toward it.

By the moonlight Curly could see that Conquering Bear was wrapped in a buffalo blanket. Only his face was showing. Curly thought it looked like the face of a dead man.

Another one of Conquering Bear's wives was following the travois.

"He will soon be better," Hump said.

Conquering Bear's wife slowly shook her head. "He doesn't eat," she said. "He will soon be half the man he was."

Raining Face had ridden up to them to see why they were there. Curly told him that his band was up ahead and wished to join with the Brulés as they headed east.

"It is a good thing," Raining Face said, "but we travel more slowly because of Conquering Bear."

"Then we shall all travel more slowly," Curly assured him.

Raining Face smiled. "I shall tell the others," he said.

Curly and Hump headed back upriver toward their band to tell them that they needed to slow down until the Brulés caught up with them.

"I am angry, Curly," Hump said. "No white man's life is worth Conquering Bear's life."

Curly nodded, but he didn't say anything. He was more confused now than ever before about all the things that had happened in the last few hours.

All the next day Curly spoke to no one. When either Little Hawk or Hump tried to talk to him, he just grunted. Finally everyone left him alone to ride at the rear of the bands as they slowly headed eastward, toward where they hoped they would never again see a white man.

On the sixth day out from Fort Laramie, the bands reached the Sand Hills, near the North Loup River, and it was decided that they would camp there for several days. Food was beginning to run low, and the Brulés were worried about Conquering Bear. His wounds had reopened, and his wives were having a difficult time stopping the bleeding.

Curly still had spoken very little to anyone since the Oglalas had joined with Conquering Bear's band. He had finally decided that he needed to seek the vision that every Sioux warrior looks for.

If he found the vision and understood its meaning, it would not only give him his adult name but would guide him for the rest of his life. What really scared Curly, though, was that not all Sioux warriors experienced these visions. What scared him even more was that he was supposed to prepare himself for this vision—but life for the Sioux was different now, and Curly was sure the Great Spirit would understand. His father, as the band's holy man, would have talked to him for many weeks, telling him how to prepare his mind to understand what the vision would tell him. He was also supposed to purify his body so it would be clean to receive the spirits. But his people were running from the white man, and there was no place to build a sweat lodge for his bath. The old ways were changing fast. He had to have his vision now. He had to learn what was happening to him and his people.

Early the next morning, before anyone was

awake, Curly rode away from the encampment. After several hours he found a small lake at the base of one of the sand hills.

This is the place, Curly thought. *This is where I shall have my vision.*

He dismounted and tethered his pony to a small bush at the lake's edge. "There is much grass here," he said to the animal. "You will not get hungry while I am gone."

Curly stripped to his breechcloth, then he started climbing the hill. Once he reached the top, he looked around until he found the perfect spot to lie down and fast until the vision came to him. Once he was prone, though, he knew that he would soon be asleep if he didn't do something to keep himself awake.

Curly stood up again and began to search the hilltop for as many sharp stones as he could find. When he thought he had enough, he took them back to where he had been lying and pushed them into the ground, so that the sharper points would dig into his back and legs. The rocks would keep him awake, he was sure.

Curly was right. He had never experienced such pain. He had heard stories about how the Crows had tortured their Sioux captives, and he wondered if what he was feeling now was like that, but then he suddenly realized that thinking of this as torture might make the spirits angry, so he refocused his mind on receiving the vision.

As the sun climbed higher and higher in the blue, cloudless sky, it slowly burned Curly's exposed skin, only adding to the pain, but he was used to this. His skin was lighter skin than the rest of the Oglalas, and he would often blister where they would only turn more brown. His lips were cracked, and his throat had never felt so dry, but still Curly lay unmoving on the sharp rocks.

It was a relief when the sun went down and

he could look up into the night sky and see the stars. He looked for familiar shapes and they gave him comfort.

When the moon appeared, Curly studied its face. For a moment he thought the face had spoken to him, and he wondered if this would be his vision, but after several minutes, when the face remained immobile, he decided that his mind had only been playing tricks on him. Anyway, the moon had already spoken to Moon Face, so Curly doubted if his vision would come that way too.

Slowly the black of the night turned to the gray of dawn, and the stars and the moon disappeared. The sun rose in the east and before long it was again burning Curly. His body ached all over.

"Have I angered you by not preparing myself properly?" Curly said, hoping the Great Spirits would hear him. "Should I have waited until I could be purified?"

The thought that he had doomed his vision now caused Curly more pain than any of the rocks that were digging into his back and legs.

When the sun was directly overhead, Curly decided that he had made a serious mistake by being so arrogant with the Great Spirit. He needed to clear his head. He needed to rethink what he was doing. As he slowly sat up, his head started to spin. He put his hand down on the ground to balance himself, but instead it struck one of the sharp rocks, which cut through the skin. Curly took it as a sign that the spirits were angry.

Finally Curly managed to stand, but, unable to keep his balance, he fell back down. Slowly he crawled to the edge of the hill.

Below him Curly saw the lake, shimmering in the midday sun. Suddenly, a sensation unlike anything he had ever felt before went through his body. The pain of the last two days disappeared. Now there was a pleasant buzzing inside his head. Curly squinted, trying to clear his vision. He was sure that there was something in the lake that was trying to surface. He closed his eyes and shook his head, thinking that maybe his mind was just playing tricks on him again, but when he opened his eyes, whatever it was was still there, and now it seemed to be motioning for him to come closer.

Curly's head had cleared enough that he managed to stand up again, but now his whole body was trembling. He put one foot on a boulder and started down the hill, but he stopped when his head began to spin once more. Curly closed his eyes. That didn't help. His head only spun faster. Still, he knew, he had to get to the lake. When he opened his eyes again, the sky above him seemed to be full of colorful clouds that were swirling even faster than the inside of his head. For a moment Curly thought it could be a prairie storm, but then just as suddenly, he knew that it wasn't.

Once again he stepped downward on a boulder to start descending the hill, but he stumbled and fell. When he tried to grab the branch of a small bush growing in between the rocks, a thorn stabbed the open wound in his palm. That caused him to jerk his hand away, and he started tumbling head over heels down the side of the hill. Frantically he clawed at the ground, trying to grasp something to break his fall, but nothing held.

Halfway down the hill, Curly landed on a little slope. He lay there, trying to get air into his lungs, but every movement of his chest caused him great pain. After a few minutes Curly turned over on his back to get his nose out of the dirt, and looked up to see a man on horseback with long brown hair floating slowly toward him. Curly thought the rider's hair looked exactly like his.

Suddenly the horse began to change

colors—some dark, some bright—colors that Curly had never seen before, even on birds or butterflies.

"I am having my vision," Curly whispered.

Curly could feel the excitement within, mingled with just a little fear that he would not be able to interpret the events unfolding before him.

As the man on the horse got closer, Curly saw that the rider's face had no war paint on it, but he did have a hawk's feather in his hair and a small brown stone tied behind one ear.

Curly had never seen a Sioux warrior who looked like this. Was the man on the horse trying to tell him that he should never look like other Sioux warriors when he went into battle?

"Speak to me," Curly whispered.

As the rider came closer, Curly could see that his eyes were clear and bright.

"You must never wear a war bonnet when

you ride against your enemies," the rider said.

"You must never paint your horse or tie up its tail before going into battle."

Curly knew that he had to store every word in his memory. He couldn't forget anything the rider said.

The rider floated closer and closer. "Before you fight your enemies, you should pick up a handful of dust from the sacred Sioux hunting ground and sprinkle some of it on your horse," he said, "then you should rub the rest of the dust into your hair and onto your body.

"After battle you must never take anything for yourself, but let your people take whatever they want," the rider continued. "You must never boast of your battles. Your people will celebrate your victories, and they will sing of your courage."

The rider stopped at the edge of the cliff. "If you do this, you will never be killed by an enemy or by a bullet," he said.

As Curly locked eyes with the man on the horse, he was sure he was looking into the world of the Sioux spirits. He had never before felt such a force, and for a minute Curly thought he would be drawn into the rider's eyes, but suddenly thunder cracked, as if the sky were about to be split in half, and lightning flashed all around him. Curly was blinded. When he finally regained his sight, the rider had floated away from the edge of the cliff.

Now the rider was surrounded by swirling ghosts of other riders. They shot arrows and bullets at him, but none of them found their mark. Some of them even disappeared when they got within inches of the man's body.

The sky got even darker. Huge drops of rain, followed by hailstones, began to pound Curly's body. He had to narrow his eyes to slits to see through the storm so he could watch the rider coming toward him. He even felt a swoosh of the air as the man passed.

Almost as fast as the storm had come up, it stopped, and with a loud scream, a red-backed hawk flew over the rider's head. Curley watched the hawk in flight until he could no longer see it, but when he turned his eyes back to where the rider had been, he was no longer there.

Just then Curly felt a hand shaking his shoulder. For a second he thought the rider had returned, but when he looked around, he saw his father.

"Where have you been, Son?" Crazy Horse demanded angrily. "You left without saying a word to anyone."

Curly was puzzled. "That is the Sioux way, Father," he said. "Hump and I have often been gone for days, learning how to survive on our own, just as our forefathers did, and you weren't angry then."

"That was before what happened at Fort Laramie. Our lives have changed, and you need to remember that," Crazy Horse countered. "Conquering Bear is dying, and you have distracted everyone from thinking about that, because we were also worried about you."

Curly bowed his head. "I'm sorry, Father," he said. "I wanted to seek my vision."

"You came to seek your vision without instruction from me first?" Crazy Horse demanded angrily. "You did this without being purified?"

"I felt I was ready," Curly said.

"Untether your pony, Curly. You will ride with me back to camp at once," Crazy Horse said. "Tonight I will ask the great Wakan Tanka to intervene with the other spirits. I hope you have not made them so angry that you won't ever have your vision."

Curly wanted to tell his father about the vision he had had, because he was sure that the spirits weren't angry with him. He was positive he had had the vision meant just for him. This wasn't the time, though.

When Curly and his father reached the camp, they heard the women wailing, and Curly knew immediately why. Conquering Bear had died. Without saying another word to Curly, Crazy Horse rode on ahead.

Curly rode to the corral and put his pony inside. Just before he reached his tipi, Hump stopped him.

"Where have you been?" Hump asked. "We thought the white soldiers had taken you."

The thought angered Curly. "No white solider will ever take me," he said.

Hump looked at him. "How do you know?" he asked. "Did you have a vision that told you?"

Curly turned away from his friend. He was in no mood to discuss what had happened to him on the hilltop. He knew what he knew, and in a few days, when his father's anger had subsided and when the mourning for Conquering Bear was over, he would approach his father about his vision, and see if his father could help him understand what it meant.

We Only Want Peace

Within a few days the warriors of the Oglala and Brulé bands had made a decision. They would avenge the death of Conquering Bear.

Spotted Tail, Curly's uncle, led a party of Brulé warriors south to the Platte River. When they returned, Curly learned that they had attacked a stagecoach on the Holy Road, killing the two drivers and one of the passengers.

Curly overheard his father talking to some of the older members of the band.

"This will anger the white soldiers even

more," Crazy Horse said. "They will seek us out here. They will not stop until they find all the Sioux and kill us."

The men nodded.

Curly didn't know what to think. Wasn't it the right of the Sioux to avenge the death of Conquering Bear? Once more he thought about how the white man's arrival was changing the lives of his people.

At noon the next day, two of his Miniconjou relatives rode into the encampment with news about what was now being called the "Grattan Massacre."

"The white soldiers are claiming that the cow was not shot for sport," Iron Tail said. "They say that we did it to lure the soldiers out of Fort Laramie, so we could kill them."

"That is not true," Crazy Horse said.

"When did the white man ever speak the truth? He only speaks what he wants to believe," Jumping Bull said. "This was the first time that white soldiers were killed on the plains, and now they are planning to strike back."

"We have avenged Conquering Bear, and we have no more quarrel with the white soldiers," Spotted Tail said. "We will move our people even farther away so they cannot attack us."

"My band will follow you," Crazy Horse said.

Curly was happy about his father's decision. He now believed that Spotted Tail was a stronger leader than Man-Afraid-of-His-Horses.

"But we must get more horses to make up for the ones we had to leave behind when we left Fort Laramie," Crazy Horse said. "If we go south, to where the Pawnees are, we can steal some of theirs."

The idea excited Curly. He hated the Pawnees almost as much as he hated the white man.

Early the next morning the new band of

Oglalas and Brulés, led by Spotted Tail, headed south along the North Loup River. That evening, when they reached a grove of trees at the river's edge, Spotted Tail said they would stop there so that the women and children could rest.

"We are far enough away from the Pawnees that if they have sent out scouts to spy on us, they will not believe we are planning to raid them," Spotted Tail said. "But tonight, after it appears we are sleeping and they have reported this back to their village, we will send some of our fastest warriors there and steal all their horses."

Curly couldn't sleep. All he could think about was getting to the Pawnee village.

Finally, when the moon was right above the hole in his tipi, Crazy Horse shook his shoulder, thinking he was asleep, and whispered, "It is time."

Without making any sound, Curly, still fully clothed, rose from his buffalo blanket, grabbed his bow and quiver, and left the tipi before his father.

Outside in the moonlight, he could see the other warriors standing near the pony corral. Even Sioux ponies had been trained not to make sounds that might alert the enemy. Quickly the men and boys mounted. Curly saw that Hump was among the ones Spotted Tail had chosen to go on the raid. Curly was glad. Even though he had not told Hump anything about his vision, Hump was still his best friend, and the time would come—perhaps on this raid—when Curly would tell his *kola* what had happened on top of the hill.

With Spotted Tail in the lead, the warriors headed out of the encampment toward the Pawnee village. The closer they got, the more excitement Curly felt, but, remembering the vision he had had, he said nothing. He was determined that no matter how many ponies he himself stole, he would keep none for himself.

Suddenly Spotted Tail stopped. "Something is wrong," he said. "The wind is from the south, which is good, because it would not carry our scent into the village, but it would carry the sound of their ponies to us, and I hear nothing."

Curly had been thinking the same thing, but he had decided that because he wasn't as experienced as the rest of the warriors, he might have missed something. As disappointed as he was at Spotted Tail's news, he was happy that his first instincts had been right.

Finally they reached the Pawnee village. As Spotted Tail had suspected, it was deserted.

"I know of an Omaha village south of here," Spotted Tail said. "We will go there and take their horses."

Curly was disappointed. A raid on the Pawnees would have been more satisfying, but a raid on the Omahas was better than nothing. The Omahas were not fierce fighters, Curly knew. Although the men sometimes hunted, just like the Sioux, they also planted crops and played musical instruments. Still, they kept horses, and the purpose of the raid was to get as many horses as they could.

Hump looked over at Curly and grinned, as the band of warriors headed toward the Omaha village between the North Loup River and Beaver Creek.

"Are you thinking about your first coup?" Hump asked.

Curly nodded solemnly. "Yes," he replied.

To a Sioux warrior, *touching* the enemy was almost as important as killing him. This was called the "counting coup." If you could ride into an enemy's village, then touch as many warriors as possible with a lance or with a bow—or even better, with your bare hand—the Sioux women would sing your praises. You would also get to wear feathers in your hair. The more enemy warriors you touched, the more feathers you wore.

But Curly remembered that in his vision the rider had only one feather in his hair.

Up ahead, Spotted Tail had halted, but Curly, lost in his daydream, almost collided with the horse in front of him. At the last minute he reined in and stopped.

"We'll cross the river here," Spotted Tail said. "The Omaha village is on the other side of that rise."

At this particular point the North Loup was barely a trickle, so the crossing wouldn't be hard, but Curly knew that the band would now be out in the open. They had approached the Omaha village from the west side of the river, because it was lined with more trees and tall grasses, giving them more cover than they would have had on the east bank.

Curly looked at the gray dawn and knew that at this hour the only people in the village who would be stirring would be the women at the cook fires. This was the best time to stage a raid. Most of the Omahas would either still be asleep or just be waking up.

Right before they reached the rise that overlooked the Omaha village, Spotted Tail motioned for everyone to dismount and crawl on their stomachs to the edge of the rise.

Curly and Hump reached the rise before most of the other warriors.

Below, Curly saw a large grove of trees along the banks. In among the trees, he saw the sod and timber houses the Omaha lived in. Smoke rising from the trees told him that the women had started preparing the morning meal. Beyond the trees, south along the banks of the North Loup, Curly saw the crops that the Omahas raised. They were in luck, though, because the corral that held the horses was on their side of the village. Curly couldn't imagine staying in one place, as the

Omahas did. He liked being a Sioux. He liked moving from one location to another.

Spotted Tail whistled like a bird, which was the signal for everyone to mount up again.

With a loud whoop from Spotted Tail, the warriors started toward the Omaha village.

As Curly and Hump approached the trees, they saw some of the Omahas sticking their heads out of their houses to see what all the noise was about. Immediately they started scattering about, running first one way and then another, trying to get to their horses, then realizing that the corral was where most of the Sioux warriors were.

Curly was racing through the village, looking for an Omaha warrior to touch, so he would have his first coup. He barely missed a boy who looked about the same age as Hump. Just as Curly reached him, the Omaha dove behind one of the huts. Quickly Curly turned his horse around for another pass through the village. This time he had to dodge the arrows of some of the Omaha warriors who had managed to recover from the surprise attack.

Curly was determined that he was not going to leave the village without touching one of the men. Angrily he raced through the village for a third time. Ahead he saw a warrior pull an arrow from a quiver and put it in his bow. Instead of veering away from the man, Curly urged his horse faster toward him. Curly saw the arrow heading his way, and he immediately thought of the rider in his vision. Curly waited until the arrow was almost to him, then leaned slightly to the right, and the arrow whizzed by, close enough that he felt the wind from it. The Omaha blinked. It was clear he had never seen anyone challenge an arrow like that. The Omaha still hadn't moved when Curly reached him. Curly's hand slapped the man's bare chest, making a loud whacking sound. Excited beyond belief at his first coup, Curly had reached the edge of the village and was prepared to make another run, when he saw something dive into the thick brush on the river bank.

Quickly he pulled an arrow from his quiver, put it in his bow, and aimed it toward the spot.

As the arrow entered the bushes, there was a loud groan. Curly knew he had hit the Omaha.

Curly raced his pony toward the bushes. When he reached the underbrush, he jumped off, and stood for a minute, listening. When there was no further sound, he began pulling the branches apart, searching for the warrior he was sure he had killed.

As Curly grabbed another branch to pull it back, his hand felt something wet. When he looked, he saw that his hand was covered with blood. Curly jerked it away from the branch. Quickly he wiped it on some leaves. Until that moment this had been a game of sorts, something that all Sioux boys dreamed up, killing an enemy in battle, but Curly had never killed anything but an animal for food, and now the thought that he would soon see a dead Omaha warrior made his stomach lurch. He forced himself to think about something else, but the rumbling in his stomach wouldn't stop.

Suddenly he saw a swatch of brightly colored cloth, and he knew that with one more separation of the branches, he would find the body of the Omaha warrior.

The Omaha was on his stomach. Curly dropped to one knee, grabbed the warrior's hair, and pulled the head up, but with a yelp he released the hair and let the head fall back onto the ground.

He had killed an Omaha woman!

Curly jumped up. Now his stomach, which he thought he had under control, was churning relentlessly. Curly bent over and gagged.

Just then Curly heard a noise behind him.

He turned quickly, wiping his mouth with one hand and grabbing an arrow from his quiver with the other.

Instead of an Omaha warrior, he was facing a member of his own raiding party, Charging Hawk.

"I saw movement," Charging Hawk said. "I thought it might be an Omaha warrior hiding in the bushes."

Curly shook his head.

Charging Hawk looked puzzled. He grabbed Curly by the shoulders and moved him aside. "You killed a *woman*?" He looked at Curly and grinned. "Couldn't you catch any of the men, little brother?"

"I didn't know," Curly managed to say.

Charging Hawk laughed. "Hurry, little brother," he said. "The Omahas have all run away, we have their horses, and we're taking whatever we can carry from inside their houses."

When Charging Hawk was gone, Curly

turned back to the woman. How could he have done this? he wondered. It didn't matter to him that it was all right to kill a woman. She reminded him of his sister. He tried to think how he would feel if a Crow or a Pawnee or someone from another tribe killed Laughing One.

Curly ran from the underbrush and jumped on his pony.

When he reached the rest of the raiding party, everyone looked at him and grinned. Curly felt like running away. Instead he busied himself with tying onto the backs of the horses what the other warriors were taking out of the Omaha huts.

"Look, Curly," Hump said. He held up some deerskin leggings. "I am taking these for myself. There were more." He nodded to a nearby hut. "You should get some too."

Curly shook his head. He would always be true to his vision, which meant he would never take anything for himself. He supposed he could take some things for his family, but right now, he didn't even feel like doing that. Anyway, he knew all of the plunder would be divided among the members of the band, so his family wouldn't miss out.

"I say we continue south and raid more of the Omaha villages," Charging Hawk said. "Their warriors are worse than women."

"No. We have more than enough for everyone," Spotted Tail said. "Now we will get our women and children, and then we'll go to the Black Hills for the winter."

Curly was pleased to hear that. The Great Spirits there would protect them from the white man, and they could spend a peaceful winter, resting and making plans for the spring.

When the warriors neared the spot where the rest of the band had camped, Spotted Tail told Curly and Hump to ride on ahead and tell the people to get ready to leave. Curly was glad to leave the band for a while.

He had had to endure a lot of teasing from the rest of the men for slaying the Omaha woman. Now he felt relieved to hear only the wind in his ears as he and Hump raced toward the encampment.

Within an hour after Curly and Hump's arrival, the camp had been taken down and packed on the travois, and the band was ready to leave. Everyone seemed happy that they would be heading back to the Black Hills, instead of south, into unfamiliar territory.

For the next two days they traveled across the plains in a northwesterly direction, toward the Black Hills. But on the third day, when the band spotted several huge herds of buffalo, Spotted Tail rode up to Crazy Horse. "I want you to tell me what you have been thinking since we first saw the buffalo herds," Spotted Tail said.

Without hesitating, Crazy Horse replied, "I believe we are being told that this is where we should stop, because there are more than enough buffalo to get us through this next winter."

Spotted Tail nodded. "Little Thunder's village is very close to here, on the banks of Bluewater Creek," he said.

"He is Brulé, and he will welcome us," Crazy Horse said. "He is a powerful and courageous chief, and he is also a friend of the white man."

"I was thinking the same thing, Holy Man," Spotted Tail said. "I will discuss this with the rest of the band."

As it turned out, most of the band wanted to join Little Thunder's band. They were tired, and they didn't want to travel any farther. Because of the huge herds of buffalo, they knew there would be enough food here, and that they might not find as much farther on. With more and more whites coming onto the plains, it was hard to tell where the buffalo herds would be.

But Curly's stepmother and sister said they wanted to continue on to the Black Hills.

"This is the time to be close to family," Gathers Her Berries told Crazy Horse. "Little Thunder's village is too near the white soldiers."

Little Hawk wanted to stay with Curly. For Curly, that was a good thing. In his heart he felt that he and Little Hawk, as Sioux warriors, should be where they could fight the white soldiers if they continued to harass his people.

"Little Hawk and I will stay with Spotted Tail," Curly said. "We will join you in the spring."

With that decided, the next morning Crazy Horse continued on toward the Black Hills with a small band. Spotted Tail led the rest of the band to Little Thunder's village.

Curly couldn't have been happier. Little Thunder welcomed their band, which almost doubled the size of the village. Now, with so many things to do, almost no one had time to tease Curly about what had happened during the raid on the Omaha village. Curly was pleased, too, that no one saw fit to tell the story to anyone in Little Thunder's band.

Within just a few hours of their arrival, Curly, Little Hawk, and Hump had joined the rest of the warriors on a buffalo hunt.

The herds of buffalo Spotted Tail's band had seen earlier were nothing compared to the herds they found on the east side of the Platte River.

"We're not far from Fort Laramie," Hump whispered to Curly and Little Hawk. "While we're hunting the buffalo, we should watch for the white soldiers, too."

Curly nodded. He didn't like the idea of being so close to the place where the Sioux's trouble had started, but if his father and Spotted Tail thought they would be safe with Little Thunder, then he would believe it.

Over the next two days Curly killed four buffalo and Little Hawk killed one, but the kill was only a part of the work that needed to be done. That was followed by the dressing of the animals and the drying of the meat. Most of the work was done by the women, but from time to time, Curly, Little Hawk, and Hump helped, if they were asked by one of the young girls.

Since the Holy Road was close by, on the other side of the Platte River, some of the warriors in the village would sometimes harass the white settlers. Not everyone in the village thought this was a good idea, but Curly agreed with the warriors who went—that they were Sioux and that they were not afraid of anyone, Crows or Pawnees or white soldiers.

Curly, Little Hawk, and Hump had only been in Little Thunder's village for a week when a white solider arrived early one morning, demanding to see the chief.

When Little Thunder came out of his tipi, Curly went to stand beside him.

"What is it you want, my friend?" Little Thunder asked.

"I bring a message from Agent Thomas Twiss, whom the Great White Father in Washington has named chief of all the Sioux people," the soldier said. "You are to come to Fort Laramie at once."

It was all Curly could do to keep from lunging at this soldier with his knife. No white man could ever be a chief of the Sioux!

"I cannot do that," Little Thunder said calmly. He motioned with his hand for the solider to look around the village, but the solider kept his eyes on Little Thunder. "As you can see, we have much work to do. When we are finished, I will be glad to come to Fort Laramie."

"Agent Twiss will be very angry if you do not come now," the soldier said. "He will think you are no longer a friend of the Great White Father."

"That isn't true. My people only want

peace," Little Thunder said, his voice remaining steady. "Tell Agent Twiss that I will come to Fort Laramie in three months, when the work here is finished."

Without another word the soldier remounted his horse and rode out of the village.

Curly went back to helping cure the buffalo hides, but he knew that what Little Thunder had told the solider would make the other soldiers angry, and now he feared for the safety of everyone in the band. He was glad his parents and his sister had decided to go on to the Black Hills.

Over the next few weeks Curly, Little Hawk, and Hump did their part to help the village prepare for the coming winter. When no trouble came from the white soldiers, Curly began to think that perhaps Little Thunder really was their friend and that if he told them he wasn't going to do something, they just left him alone.

When Hump suggested that he and Curly and Little Hawk ride out onto the prairie, away from the village, to shoot some rabbits for a stew, Curly jumped at the chance.

"I have the smell of buffalo fat inside my nose, and I can't smell anything else," Curly said. "I need to clear my head."

The three of them got their ponies from the corral, then headed east, away from the village. All day they rode. From time to time they practiced coups with one another. Hump had complained that he thought he was losing his skills as a Sioux warrior because of the restrictions the white man had put on the tribes. Finally they decided to head back to the village.

They had only ridden a couple of miles when Curly reined up. His heart was suddenly beating faster than he could ever remember. He pointed toward the western horizon. He knew right away that something was very wrong. "Smoke," he managed to say.

With Curly in the lead, the three of them raced back to Little Thunder's village. When they got there, all of the tipis and lodges had been burned to the ground, and there were bodies lying everywhere. The entire village had been destroyed.

Crazy Horse

The sight of the destroyed tipis and so many of his people lying dead in their own village filled Curly with a rage he had never known before. He knew he would never forget that sight. He knew, too, that one day, somewhere, somehow, he would avenge the deaths of so many Sioux.

Without a band of their own now, Curly, Hump, and Little Hawk started riding eastward, toward nowhere in particular. Curly knew that when they were hungry, they could stop at a friendly camp or village and they would be fed. That was the Indian way.

144

Soon, though, Curly decided that he preferred to hunt his own food and sleep under the stars—alone. Little Hawk and Hump, understanding Curly's mood, decided to head toward the Black Hills. Curly told them that when he felt the time was right, he would follow, but that until that time, he wanted to be alone.

At more and more villages, all Curly found were people who had lost hope. Their way of life was changing because the white soldiers would not let them live as they always had. Now they sat around and waited until they were told it was time to go to the nearest fort, where the soldiers would give them food and blankets and other things the president of the United States thought they needed. Curly didn't think they needed any of the white man's things. Before the white man came, the Sioux knew how to take care of themselves. Now they didn't—or didn't care—and all this made Curly very sad.

In the summer of 1857, when Curly was fifteen, he decided that it was time to go to the Black Hills to rejoin his family. From other Sioux he had met in the last few months, he learned that more and more white soldiers were coming to look for any Sioux they considered troublemakers.

"The Black Hills are home to our spirits," Curly told himself. "I want to be near them and my family."

The ride north gave Curly plenty of time to think about what he and the other Sioux should do. He knew that the white soldiers were too strong for any one small band. Whenever the soldiers fought, they attacked one Indian camp or village at a time, killing the warriors, as well as the women and children. If the Sioux were to win their battles against the white soldiers, Curly knew, they had to rethink how they fought.

Curly remembered when Conquering Bear's camp had been attacked. The white soldiers had been few, and the Sioux had been in the thousands. Curly knew that that was the secret to winning against the white soldiers. The Sioux had to join together in great numbers. Only then could they defeat the white soldiers and reclaim their land and their way of life.

Of course, he told himself, numbers alone were not enough. The white soldiers had powerful guns, some held in the hand, and some carried in wagons. It was the wagon guns that could destroy a village from a long way off. How would the Sioux ever be able to fight those? Curly wondered.

As he continued north, Curly passed houses made from sod and fences that stretched across the land, forcing him to ride around where once he had ridden straight through. Curly tried to contain his anger. He wanted to pull up every fence post he saw, but they sometimes stretched from horizon to horizon, it seemed. He knew that he would be no match for white settlers with guns.

Once, too, in the distance Curly saw a few head of buffalo, but there weren't the huge herds that used to feed and clothe his people.

As Curly got closer to the Black Hills, he began to encounter other Sioux, but it was only when Curly recognized the son of Old-Man-Afraid-of-His-Horses, called Young-Man-Afraid-of-His-Horses, that he rode over to him.

"I see you are going to Bear Butte for the Great Council of all the Sioux too," Young-Man-Afraid-of-His-Horses said.

Curly looked puzzled.

"Didn't you know about that?" Young-Man-Afraid-of-His-Horses asked.

Curly shook his head. "I have not talked to many people for some while now," he said. "I have been riding the prairie, thinking of what we Sioux can do to fight the white soldier."

"If you have thought of any ideas, then you need to come to the council," Young-Man-

Afraid-of-His-Horses told him. "That is why we are all meeting."

Curly was sure it was his vision that had told him to go to Bear Butte in the Black Hills, but he didn't say anything about it.

Curly rode the rest of the way with Young-Man-Afraid-of-His-Horses. The sight Curly saw when he came up to a ridge warmed his heart. Never before had he seen so many Sioux in once place. It was larger than the gathering at Fort Laramie. In his heart Curly knew that the Sioux should never have gone to that gathering, because it was the white man who had called it, and it was the white man who had forced the Sioux and the other tribes to agree to things they did not understand. Curly vowed that would never happen again.

Curly and Young-Man-Afraid-of-His-Horses bid each other farewell as they headed off in separate directions to find their families.

Suddenly Curly saw his *kola*. "Hump!" he shouted.

Hump, who was riding with Lone Bear, looked up and immediately broke into a grin when he saw Curly.

"My brother!" Hump shouted.

He and Lone Bear quickly rode up to Curly, and they grasped one another's arms.

"I was worried that you might not know about this council," Hump said, "and I did not know where you'd be, so I could not come look for you."

"I am here because the Great Spirit spoke to my heart," Curly said. He looked around. "This is a wonderful sight."

Hump nodded. "All the great Sioux chiefs are here, Curly," he said. "Red Cloud, Sitting Bull, Crow Feather, and Old-Man-Afraid-of-His-Horses."

"Don't forget Touch-the-Clouds, Hump," Lone Bear said.

Hump laughed. "How could I forget him?"

he said. "He is over seven feet tall. You can always see his head above everyone else's."

"It is so good to see you, but I must find my family now," Curly said. "I have missed them for so long, and I want to embrace them."

"The Oglala lodges are over there," Lone Bear said, pointing to the left. "You will find all your family in good health."

Curly headed in the direction Lone Bear had pointed, and in a few minutes he thought he recognized his family's tipi. Just then Little Hawk came out through the opening. He suddenly noticed Curly, started jumping up and down, and then disappeared back into the tipi. Within seconds Crazy Horse emerged and started running toward Curly.

Curly dismounted and ran toward his father.

When they met, they embraced each other and squeezed so hard that Crazy Horse coughed.

They released the embrace but still held

each other at arm's length, smiling and shaking their heads in disbelief as they tried to picture the person each one of them had left over two years before.

"You are so tall now, yet so slender, like a reed," Crazy Horse said. "Still, you are a warrior, my son."

"I have grown much, Father," Curly said.

"It has been two winters since your mother and I saw you," Crazy Horse said. "Are you well?"

"Yes, Father, I am well, and I am very happy to be here," Curly said.

"We were worried about you," Crazy Horse admitted in a soft voice. "Where have you been?"

"I have been many, many places," Curly said. "I have seen much that I wish to talk to you about."

"And I, too, have things I wish to talk to you about," Crazy Horse said. He put his arm around Curly and they started toward the tipi. "Tonight we will talk, and you can tell me everything that you have seen and thought for these last two years."

"I need to put my horse in the corral first," Curly said.

"There's no need for that," Crazy Horse said. "It's being taken care of."

Curly turned. He saw Hump wave to him as he led Curly's pony toward the corral. Curly waved back, then he turned around and followed his father inside the tipi.

Gathers Her Berries, Laughing One, and Little Hawk were all sitting by the fire. They had big grins on their faces. Crazy Horse and Curly took their places beside them and completed the circle.

"We wondered if we'd ever see you again," Laughing One said.

"I have been taught well," Curly said. He looked at his father. "I needed to be alone to think about our people and to try to find an answer for what is happening to them."

"And did you find that answer?" Little Hawk asked.

"I have not found all the answer, but I think I have found part of it," Curly replied, "and the image is beginning to get sharper in my head."

Over the next few days the great chiefs and warriors talked about what they should do to remain strong and to keep their land from being overrun by the towns and farms of the white settlers as they moved west.

Finally they all agreed, as Curly had understood days before, that they would have success only if they overwhelmed the white man with their numbers. They would not fight the white man alone. They would use a network of runners to warn the different camps and villages. If there was word that the soldiers were headed toward one particular village, then the closest other villages would join together to fight them.

When the bands began dispersing to

return to their villages and try to resume their lives, Curly and Crazy Horse rode off alone. Curly knew his father wanted to talk to him where they wouldn't be disturbed, and Curly had finally decided that the time had come to tell his father about his vision.

Although Crazy Horse never said anything to Curly, Curly knew that his father wanted to find just the right place for their conversation. It had to be a place where the Great Spirits were all aligned and there was no conflict going on. Finally they made camp beside a branch of the Belle Fourche River, to the north of Bear Butte. Curly thought it was one of the most peaceful places he had ever been.

They tethered their horses, then together they gathered small sticks to make a fire. Gathers Her Berries and Laughing One had packed food for them in small pouches made from buffalo hide. After the fire was going, they sat together and ate in silence.

When they finished, Crazy Horse said,

"When I first saw you, back at Bear Butte, after you had been away for two winters, I thought my eyes were deceiving me."

"Why is that, Father?" Curly asked.

"You are a full-grown man now, a true Sioux warrior," Crazy Horse said, "and there are many things that I should already have told you."

Curly tensed and looked expectantly at his father. "Is it too late now?" he asked warily.

Crazy Horse shook his head. "No, my son, it is not too late," he said.

Curly relaxed. "What do you want to tell me, Father?" he said.

"It is not easy to be a good warrior, Curly, but I have watched you for many years, and I have no fear that you will dishonor the tribe or your family or yourself," Crazy Horse began. "A Sioux warrior should always understand that the people come first. It is especially important that you take care of the old people, and that is not easy, but it is they who are the keepers of the knowledge of the Sioux people.

"You must never eat until after everyone else has eaten. If there is no food left, then you will be hungry that night, and on your next hunt, you should kill a little more, but never so much that you waste what the Great Spirits have given us.

"When you capture horses from our enemies, you will give all of them to the people, except the ones you keep for hunting and for riding into battle."

Curly waited for his father to continue, but he sat in silence for several minutes and then suddenly stood up.

Curly stood up too. "Did you hear something, Father?" he asked.

"No," Crazy Horse said. "It is time to build a sweat lodge, so that you can purify yourself." He looked at Curly. "When we have done that, then I want to hear about what happened to you on that hill on the day Conquering Bear died."

Curly hung his head.

Crazy Horse walked over and lifted Curly's chin with the palm of his hand. "It is important to set things right with Wakan Tanka, Curly. After a sweat bath, after you have been purified, then you will see clearly those things you need to see to be a good warrior. When you tell me about your vision, you will now see it through different eyes."

Together Crazy Horse and Curly gathered several branches and arranged them in the shape of a dome by planting the ends in the soft ground and then bending the tops of the branches toward one another and tying them together.

The dome was covered by skins that Crazy Horse had tied in bundles and carried on the back of his horse.

"You must dig a hole for the stones in the center of the floor, Curly," Crazy Horse said, "but make sure it isn't too deep."

Crazy Horse found several large stones

along the creek bank and carried them back to the sweat lodge. He placed them on the fire, so they would be heated.

When Curly had finished digging the hole for the stones, he helped Crazy Horse find some sage to cover the ground around the hole. Finally Crazy Horse decided that the stones were hot enough, so he and Curly, using strong forked branches to carry them, put the stones in the hole.

While Crazy Horse filled a buffalo pouch with water from the creek, Curly took off all his clothes except a breechcloth and entered the sweat lodge. When Crazy Horse returned, he also stripped to his breechcloth and went into the lodge. He poured the water onto the hot rocks, causing the lodge to be filled with steam.

As the steam swirled up and around Curly and Crazy Horse, Crazy Horse said several prayers of purification. When he finished, he turned to Curly and said, "Now you may tell me."

Curly started tentatively, but once he'd begun, everything poured out of him, and he could feel his entire body relaxing, as he was finally able to talk to someone about his vision.

When Curly finished, Crazy Horse was silent, and Curly was sure that he was angry, but then he said, "You are the man in your vision, Curly, and you must obey everything you were told."

"I shall always do that, Father," Curly said. "I promise."

Two days later Curly, Hump, and Little Hawk decided to ride in search of new horses for the tribe. They rode farther west than any of the Oglalas had ever gone before, all the way to the Wind River.

Early one morning they came upon an Arapaho village, where there were lots of wonderful horses.

"We must take these back to our people,"

Curly said. "These are some of the most magnificent horses I have ever seen."

"I see several I want for myself," Hump said.

"So do I," Little Hawk agreed.

Curly didn't say anything. He remembered how he needed to obey his vision by not taking anything for himself.

While Hump and Little Hawk put on war paint, Curly tied a small brown stone behind his ear, fastened a hawk's feather in his hair, and threw a handful of dust over his horse and himself.

Suddenly the Arapahos spotted them, but Curly could tell that they were surprised to see Sioux warriors so far from their hunting ground.

Curly, Hump, and Little Hawk began circling the Arapaho village, whooping and hollering, shooting their arrows under their horses' necks, but the Arapaho managed to hold them off.

Then Curly galloped straight into the

Arapaho village, once again, taking the enemy by surprise. Arrows and bullets were flying all around him, but none of them came even close, and more than once Curly remembered the rider in his vision. Several times he touched Arapaho warriors with his bare hand in counting coups.

When he reached Hump and Little Hawk, he had a big grin on his face.

"I'm going in again," Curly said, "then we'll take the horses."

Curly raced into the village. He saw two Arapaho warriors standing at the edge of a tipi, but just as he reached them, they raced out to try to stop him. Curly shot both of them with arrows. Without thinking, he leaped from his horse and scalped the two Arapahos. As Curly lifted their scalps for Hump and Little Hawk to see, in the way that Sioux warriors proved how many enemy warriors they had killed, an Arapaho arrow struck his leg. Curly's horse bolted, and he had to run to safety at the edge of the village, where Hump and Little Hawk were waiting for him.

Hump quickly cut the iron-tipped arrow out of Curly's leg. Little Hawk handed him a piece of skin which he had taken from one of the dead Arapaho horses and Hump wrapped it around Curly's wound.

"I forgot!" Curly said angrily. "I forgot!"

"What did you forget?" Little Hawk asked.

Curly shook his head. He didn't want to let anyone know that he had forgotten that he wasn't supposed to take anything for himself in a raid, even an enemy's scalp. In doing so, he had destroyed the magic that surrounded him in battle.

I shall never forget again, Curly thought.

Little Hawk had also caught Curly's horse, so he helped his brother onto it and said, "Can we still get some of the horses?"

Curly nodded. The Arapahos were now inside their tipis, waiting, Curly thought, for another run through, but instead, the three of them raced for the corrals, where they herded out as many horses as they thought they could manage on the way back to their camp.

When they finally returned, they were honored by a victory dance. Hump and Little Hawk each stepped into the circle and sang songs of their deeds. The chief and the warriors, the women and the children, and the old men, who now only dreamed of what they once did, all shouted and cheered as they listened to the stories Hump and Little Hawk told.

Curly stayed in the shadows. When several members of the tribe tried to push him into the circle, he quickly backed out. He had already disobeyed his vision once, and for that he had received the tip of an arrow in his leg. He would not disobey the vision by bragging about his deeds in battle.

On the other hand, Crazy Horse was not

bound to Curly's vision. He could brag about his son as much as he wanted to, and the Great Spirit would not get angry. For several days Crazy Horse walked around the village singing Curly's praises. Finally Crazy Horse called everyone in the village together.

"From this day on, I shall have a new name. I shall be called Worm," Crazy Horse said. "As is our tradition, my son will have the name of his father, of my father, and of my father's father. He will be called 'Crazy Horse.'"

Our Sacred Land

The years following the council at Bear Butte were almost like a return to the old days for the Sioux. For the most part they weren't bothered by the white soldiers, because the United States was struggling with problems that would eventually lead to the Civil War. No one paid much attention to the Sioux or to any of the other Indians of the northern plains.

With their new chief, Black Shield, Crazy Horse's band followed the buffalo herds from the Black Hills to the Powder River, clashing from time to time with their old enemies, the Crows and the Shoshones. Crazy Horse soon became a popular leader of these expeditions. Not only was he an expert horseman, but the arrows he shot never missed their marks. What's more, the arrows of the Crows and Shoshones never even came close to striking him. Crazy Horse was now accompanied not only by Hump, Lone Bear, and Little Hawk, but also by warriors from several other bands. They all wanted to share in Crazy Horse's powerful magic.

During tribal hunts Crazy Horse killed more buffalo than anyone else. From time to time he also shot deer, elk, and antelope, all of which he gave to the people in his band who couldn't hunt for themselves: the wives of warriors who had been slain in battle and the old people.

Still, Crazy Horse was happiest when he was hunting with Worm. They would ride out together on the prairie, sometimes staying away for days at a time. These trips were as much about father and son being together as they were about getting more food for the band.

It was now late autumn, 1858, and the band had seen fewer buffalo than everyone expected. Crazy Horse knew that winter was just a few weeks away. It was soon clear to him that instead of feasting so well for so many weeks, as his band had done, they should have dried more meat to get ready for the winter.

After several days of looking, Crazy Horse and Worm had finally found a valley full of grazing buffalo, but Worm said they weren't ready to be killed yet, because their coats weren't thick enough. Worm said that the band would need to follow the herd until it was ready to be killed.

"I shall return to our village," Worm told Crazy Horse. "You stay with the herd, so we will know where it is."

It would never have occurred to Crazy

Horse to argue with or contradict his father. Crazy Horse knew that no matter how old he got, he would always be able to learn from what his father told him. He knew the reason Worm didn't think they should kill any of this herd now had to do with the balance of nature. That was very important to the life of all the creatures Wakan Tanka had placed on the earth. Now this balance was even more important, as the white man continued to kill more and more of the buffalo, removing them from the Sioux hunting grounds so that the white farmers could tear up the land with their plows and plant their crops. What skill did it take to drop a few seeds into the earth and sit back and watch them grow? Crazy Horse wondered. Eventually whoever did that became weak because it dulled his senses. The Omahas were planters, and Crazy Horse remembered how their warriors had scattered like women during the Sioux raid.

Worm and the rest of the band finally returned to the valley, but when some of the warriors rode to the other side to form a ring around the herd, they discovered several white soldiers camped there. Two of the warriors rode back to inform Black Shield.

"We will tell them to leave," Black Shield said. "If they do not heed our warnings, we will kill them."

Crazy Horse and Hump ran to the corral to get their horses, then they joined Black Shield, Worm, and Tall Eagle for the ride across the valley to the soldiers' camp.

It took them a couple of hours, because they circled around the herd of buffalo to keep them from stampeding.

When they arrived at the camp, Crazy Horse saw that the other Sioux warriors had the soldiers surrounded.

"You have no right to be here. The Black Hills are sacred to the Sioux," Black Shield

told the soldiers. "If you do not leave at once, you will make the spirits angry."

One of the men stepped forward. "I'm Lieutenant Warren," he said. "We can't leave until we've surveyed this land. That's all we're doing. With the survey we'll be able to make maps of this part of the country."

"Why do you need to do that? This is Sioux land," Black Shield said. "No white men are supposed to be here."

"We told the white soldiers that we Sioux would not attack settlers on the Holy Road. We told them, too, that we would not attack settlers on the road from Fort Laramie to Fort Pierre," Crazy Horse said. "We have kept our word, but you have not kept your word."

"How is that true?" Lieutenant Warren asked.

"If you make maps, it will be easy for other white settlers to come here," Worm said. "They will know the way."

Lieutenant Warren was silent for a few minutes, then he nodded. "Yes, you're right," he said. "They will know the way."

"When they come, they will kill the buffalo, and they will dig up the land," Crazy Horse said. "The Great Spirits will be angry with us for letting this happen, and we will be forced to wander until we starve to death."

"If I return without a map, the Great White Father will be angry with me and with you," Lieutenant Warren said. "Why don't you just let me finish, and when I see the Great White Father, I'll tell him what you said."

"No maps!" Black Shield shouted.

"No maps!" the other Sioux warriors repeated.

Lieutenant Warren gulped. He took a deep breath. "All right," he said. "We'll return to Fort Laramie at once."

Black Shield shook his head. "You cannot go in that direction," he said.

Lieutenant Warren looked puzzled. "Why

not?" he asked angrily. "That's where we came from."

Black Shield turned to Crazy Horse. "You tell him," he said. "I am tired of talking to him."

Crazy Horse was pleased that Black Shield thought enough of his knowledge that he allowed him to do this. "There is a large herd of buffalo there," Crazy Horse said. "If you go that way, you will frighten them, and that could mean our people will starve to death this winter."

Lieutenant Warren's shoulders slumped. Crazy Horse could tell that he and the other soldiers were now frightened that the Sioux would not let them leave the area alive.

"What do you suggest we do, then?" Lieutenant Warren asked in a quiet voice.

Crazy Horse lifted his arm and pointed north. "Ride to Bear Butte, then turn to the east, so that you can circle around the Black Hills and head back west," he said. "It will take you several more days to reach Fort

Laramie, but it will mean that you will not bother the buffalo."

Lieutenant Warren nodded. "My men and I will leave first thing in the morning," he said.

Crazy Horse shook his head. "You must leave now," he said. "You are not supposed to be here, and the longer you are here, the angrier the spirits will be."

Lieutenant Warren closed his eyes and let out his breath. "My men and I will leave at once."

The soldiers scrambled around faster than Crazy Horse thought they could, getting their belongings strapped onto the backs of their horses and into the one wagon they had with them, and started north toward Bear Butte.

Tall Eagle and the warriors Black Shield had originally sent to this side of the valley began setting up their camp.

As Crazy Horse watched the last of the

white soldiers disappear over the horizon, he knew it would only be a matter of time before the Black Hills were no longer the sacred land of the Sioux.

The Old Ways

As the year 1861 dawned, Crazy Horse was nearing his twentieth birthday, and he began to believe that perhaps the Sioux had finally convinced the white man to leave them alone and let them return to their old ways. After Lieutenant Warren and his soldiers took their surveying equipment and left the Black Hills almost three years before, no one else came, either soldiers or settlers, to disturb the sacred land. Without having this worry to distract them, the Sioux continued doing what really mattered in life for them: hunting, and fighting the Crows and the Shoshones.

Crazy Horse never could really understand why he enjoyed being alone so much, but he did, and he would ride for days on the endless prairie, thinking, or stalking a deer or some other game.

Sometimes when Crazy Horse had been away for long periods of time, he would often arrive back at his camp, as he had this day, just in time to join one of the raiding parties.

"We're going to raid a Shoshone village," Hump whispered to him. "We need their horses!"

The rest of the camp had gathered to sing the warriors' praises. The songs were the loudest for Crazy Horse.

The people sang of the deer he had brought to the old woman that fed her through the winter.

They sang of the horses he had brought to the old man who wanted them for his last journey to the land of the Great Spirit.

They sang of all his counting coups against the Crows and the Shoshones and the Pawnees and the Omahas.

They were still singing when the raiding party left the camp.

Crazy Horse found it difficult to be around people too long when they were praising him. He did what he did because he thought it was the right thing to do. He didn't do it for glory. He knew it was the Sioux way to sing the praises of the tribe's warriors, but he was always ready to be left alone. Even as he traveled with the raiding party, he was at its edge, never in the middle with the others, laughing and joking and boasting of what they were planning to do.

After two days they finally reached the Shoshone village and headed straight for the corral. Using their expert horsemanship, Crazy Horse, Little Hawk, and Hump easily managed to head the lead stallion in the

direction they wanted him to go, which meant that the rest of the horses in the herd would follow.

The raiding party had the herd halfway up a hill by the time Chief Washakie and the rest of the Shoshone warriors realized what was happening. Crazy Horse knew they would be too busy trying to save the remaining horses to follow the Oglalas right away, but as soon as they could, Crazy Horse was sure the Shoshones would come after them.

Crazy Horse, Little Hawk, and Hump agreed to stay behind to make sure that the Shoshones didn't get their horses back. They were successful. After a short battle the Shoshones were defeated.

Crazy Horse, Little Hawk, and Hump raced away in the direction of the raiding party. A day later they reached the herd. Looking at the horses in it, their shiny coats gleaming in the sun, Crazy Horse knew that the raid had been worth it. His band of people would have fine horses when they got back to their camp, and for the rest of the trip he would content himself with thinking about that.

Reservations

Crazy Horse was known far and wide as a fearless warrior. He fought many battles and counted many coups. In 1866 he helped lure Captain William J. Fetterman and his eighty soldiers from Fort Phil Kearny (in what is now the northern part of Wyoming) into a trap set by other Sioux, Cheyenne, and Arapaho warriors. All eighty soldiers were killed. The Sioux called it the Battle of the Hundred Slain. The whites forever referred to it as the Fetterman Massacre.

Because of such deeds as this, Crazy Horse

was a Sioux war leader by his mid-twenties, but it was actually a role that made him uncomfortable, because he never sought the status that went with the honor.

According to Sioux tradition, the members of the different bands voted on which warriors they wanted to be their leaders. They based their opinions on each warrior's personal qualities, his virtues, and his actions. Everyone in the Sioux nation knew that Crazy Horse was a courageous warrior, but away from the warpath, he was a quiet, humble, and caring person. Crazy Horse dressed plainly, and he seldom spoke in public or participated in tribal ceremonies. Although this was not the usual custom of Sioux warriors, these qualities were much admired by members of the tribe. Crazy Horse became one of the youngest warriors ever to receive the highest honor given to a Sioux man: He became a "shirt wearer."

A shirt wearer was supposed to be a warrior who helped provide food and clothing for the members of the tribe and who protected them from their enemies. A shirt wearer was also supposed to lead the kind of life every other member of the tribe would look to as an example of what a Sioux should be.

Unfortunately the days of the Great Sioux Nation were coming to an end, and there was very little that Crazy Horse or anyone else could do about it.

Crazy Horse's best friend, Hump, was killed in 1870. The two of them had been raiding a Shoshone village when Hump was surrounded by angry enemy warriors. Crazy Horse managed to escape, but he was devastated by the loss of his *kola*. Still, he managed to get on with his life, knowing that Hump would now be hunting with the warrior spirits.

Crazy Horse had never married, although he had courted Black Buffalo Woman, a girl he had loved since childhood. But she had married Bad Face, and they now had three children. When Black Buffalo Woman realized that she was still in love with Crazy Horse, she decided to leave her husband and her children and elope with Crazy Horse. This was something that Sioux custom allowed. Angry, Bad Face went after them and almost killed Crazy Horse. Finally Black Buffalo Woman returned to her husband and children, mainly to avoid any further bloodshed. The next year Crazy Horse married Black Shawl. She bore him his only child, a daughter named They-Are-Afraid-of-Her. Two years later the baby died of cholera.

In the summer of 1872 Crazy Horse joined with Sitting Bull to try to keep the whites from building a railroad through the Sioux hunting grounds. Together with their warriors, they attacked the survey party. Finally the railroad men left, but they returned the next summer under the protection of Lieutenant Colonel George Armstrong Custer.

This time the Sioux were unable to stop what they called the "iron horse."

Even though the Sioux had lost almost all their hunting grounds, they still had their sacred Black Hills. But in 1874, when Custer sent a report to Washington, D.C., that the hills were full of gold, miners and prospectors started arriving by the thousands. The Sioux were overwhelmed. The government tried to buy the Black Hills from the Sioux, but when the chiefs refused to sell, secret meetings were held in Washington where it was decided to move all the Sioux out of the area and onto reservations.

The Battle of the Little Bighorn

In 1876 Crazy Horse led bands of Sioux and Cheyenne warriors against the U.S. Army in two of what were considered the most important battles of "the Indian Wars."

In the years prior to the battles, many of the Sioux, Cheyenne, and Arapaho bands had refused to be confined to reservations the government in Washington had set aside for them in what is today South Dakota. An 1868 treaty had promised any Indian tribe that signed it that they would be allowed to hunt the buffalo herds on the upper Missouri

River. The "nontreaty" Indians were banned from doing this. But during the summer months, the "treaty" Indians were often joined in the hunts by some of their non-treaty relatives who, in addition to hunting buffalo, also raided peaceful tribes and white settlements. The United States government responded to the problem by ordering all of the nontreaty Indians to the reservations by January 31, 1876. The order declared that any Indian who refused would be considered hostile and subject to military action.

The nontreaty Indians ignored the warning and refused to go to the reservations. Crazy Horse became the main leader of the resistance. He gathered a force of over one thousand Sioux and Cheyennes and fought back General George Crook on June 17, 1876, as Crook tried to advance up Rosebud Creek toward Sitting Bull's encampment on the Little Bighorn River.

After the victory at Rosebud Creek, Crazy

Horse and his men joined up with Sitting Bull. On June 25 and 26, Crazy Horse led the attack from the north and the west, while Hunkpapa chief Gall led the attack from the south and the east, that destroyed Lieutenant Colonel George Armstrong Custer's Seventh Cavalry. The Battle of Little Bighorn was the greatest military disaster suffered by the United States Army in all the Indian Wars.

After the battle, Crazy Horse, Gall, and Sitting Bull decided that there had been enough killing. Sitting Bull and Gall retreated to Canada, but Crazy Horse led his people back to the Black Hills, where he was sure they would be safe.

The End of the Struggle

The following autumn and on into the winter, Crazy Horse and the other Indians who had not fled to Canada were pursued relentlessly by Colonel Nelson A. Miles and the Fifth Infantry of the U.S. Army. The soldiers soon began to wear down the different bands by making it difficult for them to get food.

Some of the Indians tried hit-and-run strikes against the soldiers, but the army, using its heavy artillery, easily kept them at bay.

On January 8, 1877, Crazy Horse, with

almost a thousand warriors, led a surprise attack against Miles and his men at Wolf Mountain on the Tongue River in what is today the southern part of Montana. Unbeknownst to Crazy Horse, General Miles had hidden his cannons in wagons and when Crazy Horse and his men attacked, the soldiers opened fire. Crazy Horse called for his men to retreat to the safety of the mountain bluffs. Luckily, when Miles attacked them there, the Indians were able to escape under the cover of a heavy snowstorm.

Crazy Horse's band was tired and had no food. Now he had to make a decision he didn't want to make. More and more of the Plains Indians were surrendering, so when General Crook sent Crazy Horse a message through Chief Red Cloud that if he surrendered, his people would be given a reservation of their own on the Powder River, he agreed to Crook's terms. On May 5, 1877, Crazy Horse led his band to Fort Robinson on the Red Cloud Reservation in what is today northwestern Nebraska.

Although the reservation that Crazy Horse and his people had been promised never materialized, the band decided to remain on the Red Cloud Reservation. But Crazy Horse's presence caused unrest among the Indians and made the whites there suspicious. The older chiefs, especially, resented the attention Crazy Horse received from the younger warriors. But Crazy Horse paid little attention to what was going on around him. When General Crook requested that Crazy Horse go to Washington, D.C., to meet with President Rutherford B. Hayes, he refused.

When Crazy Horse's wife, Black Shawl, became sick, he decided to take her back to her family, but when Crook found out that Crazy Horse had left the fort against his orders, he sent soldiers to bring him back.

Crazy Horse agreed to return, and on September 6, 1877, he was taken back to

Fort Robinson. Shortly after his arrival he realized that he was actually being arrested and taken to the stockade. When he resisted, he was bayoneted in the abdomen by one of the soldiers. He died that night.

Crazy Horse's father and stepmother were given his body, and, following their son's request, they buried him in a secret place in the Black Hills.

As a leader Crazy Horse always thought of his people first. He provided them with food, clothing, and shelter, and he protected them from their enemies. He never signed any treaties that gave away Sioux land, and he only surrendered because he didn't want his people to die from hunger and cold.

For More Information

TO READ

Ambrose, Stephen E.
  *Crazy Horse and Custer: The Parallel
  Lives of Two American Warriors.*
  New York: Random House, 1975.

Blevins, Win.
  Stone Song: A Novel of Crazy Horse.
  New York: Forge, 1995.

Bruchac, Joseph.
  Crazy Horse's Vision.
  New York: Lee & Low Books, 2000.

Chiaventone, Frederick J.
  *A Road We Do Not Know: A Novel of
    Custer at the Little Bighorn.*
  New York: Simon & Schuster, 1996.

Clark, Robert A., ed.
  The Killing of Chief Crazy Horse.
  Lincoln: University of Nebraska Press, 1976.

Dugan, Bill.
  Crazy Horse.
  New York: HarperCollins Publishers, 1992.

Freedman, Russell.
  The Life and Death of Crazy Horse.
  New York: Holiday House, 1996.

Hardorff, Richard G., ed.
  *The Death of Crazy Horse: A Tragic
    Episode in Lakota History.*
  Lincoln: University of Nebraska Press, 1998.

Santella, Andrew.
  The Lakota Sioux.
  New York: Children's Press, 2001.

Sandoz, Mari.
  Crazy Horse: The Strange Man of
    the Oglalas.
  New York: Knopf, 1942.

WEB SITES

www.crazyhorse.org
www.lakhota.com
www.pbs.org/weta/thewest/people/a_c/crazy
  horse.htm
www.indians.org/welker/crazyhor.htm